THE FALL OF
KELVIN
WALKER

Other works by Alasdair Gray:

LANARK
UNLIKELY STORIES, MOSTLY
1982 JANINE

THE FALL OF KELVIN WALKER

Alasdair Gray

GROVE PRESS/*New York*

Published by Grove Press, Inc.
920 Broadway
New York, N.Y. 10010

Published in the United States in 1986 by George Braziller,
Inc. First published in Scotland in 1985 by Canongate
Publishing Ltd.

Library of Congress Cataloging-in-Publication Data

Gray, Alasdair.
  The fall of Kelvin Walker.

  I. Title.
[PR6057.R3264F3   1987]   823'.914   87–182
ISBN 0–802–13004–6

Manufactured in the United States of America

First Evergreen Edition 1987

10 9 8 7 6 5 4 3 2 1

for
Mora,
at long last,
a book
by her brother
which
will
not
make
her blush.

TABLE OF
CONTENTS

"In the beginning was the Word,
and the Word was with God,
and the Word was God."

from Saint John's
GOSPEL

❏

"My lady,
there are few more impressive sights in the world
than a Scotsman on the make."

from Sir James Barrie's
WHAT EVERY WOMAN KNOWS

1
THE
DISCOVERY
OF LONDON

One bright fresh summer morning, in a prosperous decade between two disastrous economic depressions, a thin young man disembarked in Victoria Coach Station from one of the buses plying between Scotland and London. He wore a black homburg, a black double-breasted overcoat, a celluloid collar and a tartan tie; his shoes were slightly worn but beautifully polished, and the visible parts of his legs were clad in thick woollen stockings whose tops were hidden by the coat. His lank hair had a side parting and sloped across his brow in the style of Adolf Hitler, and he stood in the warm grey early morning air holding a battered suitcase and looking around with a blank, nearly characterless face while other passengers hurried past to the refreshment room or to waiting friends. Suddenly his expression grew grimly purposeful. He walked to a stationery kiosk and said to the woman behind the counter, "I would like, please, a cheap ball-point pen, a small hard-covered pocket notebook, a street map of London and a guide to your transport system."

"You can have them, son," she answered in a Scottish voice. He relaxed and when she had got the articles together he indicated a row of newspapers and asked on a more intimate note, "Which of these advertise good jobs?"

She handed him a paper which he glanced through then carefully refolded and returned, saying, "I'll be frank with you. I'd like a paper which offers better jobs than these."

She smiled and said, "What about *The Times*?"

He looked through *The Times* then nodded, paid for his purchases and pocketed all but the map, which he unfolded and brooded over thoughtfully before leaving the station.

No one seeing him guessed that he was gripped by a gigantic excitement and had no idea where he was going. He believed he was "just getting to know the place." His quick scissoring stride suggested a determined man with no time to waste, his tight mouth and straight stare portrayed a total indifference to surroundings, yet the streets brought continually into the centre of his eye or carried past the corners of it sights which struck and intoxicated: new huge unfamiliar buildings, famous old ones recognized from films and newsphotos, girls and women dressed and decorated with a wealth and wildness and nonchalance he had never seen before in his life. The excitement went to his legs. He had eaten nothing that morning and had hardly slept on the journey down, but the thought of sitting in a restaurant was impossible. Several times he entered a bakery or sweet shop then walked forth from it eating a pie or bar of chocolate. His only other pauses were to look at the map.

Crossing Trafalgar Square for the third time that afternoon he sat suddenly on a bench near a fountain and tried to subdue his excitement by turning it into thoughts. London was wealthy. Other British cities, Glasgow for example (he had seen Glasgow) had been built by money and still contained large amounts of it, but money seemed a slower substance in the north—a powerful substance, certainly, but stolid. Those owning it had not been liberated by it. Their faces were as severe, their mouths as grimly clenched as those without. But here in London— had it happened a year ago or a century or many centuries?—money had accumulated to a point where it had flashed into wealth, and wealth was free, swift, reckless, mercuric. He could feel it humming behind the ancient and modern facades, throbbing under the streets like silver-electric sap or semen. The ornate fountains, ostentatiously squandering great cataracts of public water, symbolized it. The day was warm but freshened by sudden little windy gusts which tossed fountainspray like handfuls of coin into a by-passing crowd of men and women whom only wealth could have made so well-dressed, sure of themselves and careless. He examined the map once again. He felt sufficiently familiar now with the rough triangle of streets between Marble Arch, Westminster Abbey and St Paul's and that was something gained, but with half the day gone he had not found lodgings yet.

"That should have been your first aim," he told himself sternly. "Let it be your next. But now it would be sensible to drink something warm."

He found a small café on the Charing Cross Road and went inside. Most customers were at tables by the open door. He ordered tea and sandwiches at the counter and sat in the quiet interior. The one other person there was a stout not quite middle-aged

man, wearing casual clothes of the best quality and
smoking a cigarette with an air of such perfectly
relaxed inattention that the new arrival could only
justify himself against it by becoming businesslike.
He folded *The Times* open at the Situations Vacant
page and read it carefully, underlining desirable jobs
while devouring sandwiches and tea with steady
mechanical bites and sips. Later he opened the notebook and copied names and addresses into it. A girl
passed him carrying a coffee cup and sat at the stout
man's table. It was impossible not to distinctly see
her, even from the corner of an eye, for she was
coloured like a traffic sign: white boots, black jeans,
white shirt, a pale face with dark eyes and long black
hair. Her voice was clear and curt and could have
been called emotionless if the quick utterance had
not suggested a wish to evade emotion. The newcomer had heard her accent before on BBC radio
plays. He pressed the end of the pen against his
underlip and looked at her, frowning thoughtfully
to convey that he was considering something inside
himself. She had a beautiful, rather thin bony face
and was saying, "I believe I owe you an apology,
Mike."
The stout man stubbed out his cigarette in the ashtray and mildly murmured, "Oh, I don't think so."
"Was I stinking drunk?"
"You were pretty pissed."
"And I don't suppose Jake helped much."
"You know Jake better than I do. How is he now?"
"Still in bed. It was decent of you to get us home."
"That's what a car's for, after all. How's the head?"
"Oh, better. I woke about dawn and was sick as a
pig into the chair beside the bed." (She giggled.)
"That helped quite a lot."

The newcomer stared down at his notebook, so confused that he almost wished not to hear more. He came from a place where girls who got drunk were ill-educated and despised. This girl had not the manner of one who could be despised. She was saying, "Did you undress me, by the way?"

"Afraid not."

"Oh good. I must have done it myself."

The stout man looked at his wrist watch.

"Well, Jake certainly couldn't have done it. Look I've got to go now. You've not forgotten tomorrow night, have you?"

She said, "If you haven't changed your mind about us."

The stout man stood up saying, "I'll always love you two, no matter how alcoholic you get. See you about nine then."

"Do we bring our own bottles, Mike?"

"Not if you're broke."

"That's good because we will be."

The stout man put a hand inside his jacket pocket.

"Do you want a loan?"

"Not now. I'll come to you when I'm desperate, shall I?"

"Yes, do that. Well, have fun," said the man, and left.

The girl sipped coffee then sucked daintily at the end of her thumb. The newcomer was gripped by a spasm of determination. He stood, pocketed paper and notebook, stepped over to Mike's empty chair, laid his hat carefully on the table and sat down. The girl seemed not to notice. He placed his elbows on the table, interlocked his fingers, cleared his throat and said sharply, "Do you mind if I engage you in conversation?"

She smiled and said, "Why not? I suppose we met at the party last night."

He sternly shook his head.

"Well, I suppose it was some other party."

"No."

After a slight pause she said coldly, "I see. Well, don't let it worry you. Engage me in conversation."

This invitation was exactly what he had hoped for. He relaxed at once and started talking in an eager voluble way.

"Thank you. I'd like to begin by being honest with you. I'm a stranger here. I first arrived in London at eight o'clock this morning; I know nobody in this city and to be perfectly frank with you—"

She said, "You haven't any money."

He was puzzled.

"Why do you think that?"

"I find most strangers who start by being perfectly honest and frank go on to borrow money."

He was impressed.

"Is that so? I'm very glad you told me. That's a very handy thing to know. But—" he brightened— "as a matter of fact I have a great deal of money."

He brought a wallet from an inner pocket, laid it on the table between them and tapped it with a finger. "I think you'd be surprised at how much money I've got in this wallet."

She nodded twice and said, "I see. And you think you've found a girl who can give you a nice time."

He paused, puzzled, then suddenly blushed pink. He grabbed the wallet and stood up, speaking wildly, almost tearfully.

"I . . . I see I have pushed my company and conversation on to somebody who does not want them. I hope you will believe though that I did ... I did not mean anything insulting towards you. I'm really sincerely very sorry for my rudeness."

In her own way the girl grew equally upset. She said, "Oh Hell. Look, do sit down. Please sit down."

"But ..."

"No, please! I've just realized you're much more foreign than I thought. I'll feel hellish if you go now."

"Are you sure of that?"

"Yes, I promise. I just didn't understand."

Completely reassured he sat down and at once resumed his bright and eager manner, saying, "Where were we?"

"You were going to be frank about something."

"True. Well, when I came out of the bus station I went for a lengthy stroll through your city centre, in order to acquaint myself with it, and eventually found this place. I noticed that the people near the door, if not beautiful, were definitely artistic. So I came in and overheard you talking to that man who went out a few minutes back, and it struck me from your conversation that you are the sort of person I've come to London to meet. I am from Glaik. Have you heard of Glaik?"

"No. Tell me about it. Is it a small place?"

"No, it's big. We manufacture fish-glue and sweaters and process a lot of cheese. Some folk think the Americans were the first people to process cheese. In a way that's true, but it was a Glaik man, Murdoch Stairs, who discovered the process. And Hector McKellar, who arranges things for television, is a Glaik man, so you see that, geographically speaking, Glaik is more than a dot on the map. But culturally, it lacks scope. It was the lack of scope that made me leave it. Have you read Nietzsche?"

"Who?"

"Frederick Nietzsche, the German thinker."

"No."

"But you've heard him discussed?"

"Maybe. I'm not sure."

He shook his head, not quite convinced. He said, "That's queer. From your conversation I'd have sworn you read Nietzsche. Your conversation has what I would call a Nietzschean flavour to it. Anyway, I can talk to you about him without embarrassment. It is no exaggeration to say that in Glaik there was *nobody*, *nobody* I could discuss Neitzsche with. Nobody."

She asked sympathetically, "What do people discuss in Glaik?"

"Sport. Sport and religion. But they don't really discuss them, they fight about them. There are no thinkers or artists in Glaik. Are you an artist?"

"I'm afraid not."

"Funny. You look artistic. Do you know any artists?"

"Well, my boyfriend is a painter."

He was delighted.

"I knew you had something to do with art! Is he a good painter?"

"I couldn't say. I don't know much about painting. His friends all think he's a rotten painter. Are you an artist?"

The question shocked him.

"Me? No! I have no artistic talent at all, I'm glad to say. But where there are plenty of artists people are generally open to new ideas, especially Nietzschean ideas, and it is by these that I mean to succeed."

"Succeed in what?"

"The means are unimportant. I don't care how I begin."

He tapped the side of his brow with his index finger and said solemnly, "I've got it all worked out in here."

"What have you got worked out?" she asked, puzzled.

He suddenly smiled very widely indeed. He said genially, "This conversation is carrying us into dangerously deep water. Do you mind if I ask you your name?"

"Not at all. Jill."

"And your surname?"

"I'd rather not talk about that. It's rather sordid."

"I don't understand. How can a name be sordid?"

Jill sighed slightly then told him rapidly, but without irritation, that when her mother got divorced she had taken back her maiden name and made Jill take it too, because the mother could not bear to hear Jill's father's name mentioned. Then the mother married again and made Jill take her stepfather's name to make her seem one of the family. But Jill disliked her stepfather so her friends just called her Jill. This information made the stranger open his mouth and eyes very wide. For a moment he seemed about to blush again but said with a great air of discovery, "That is very sad!"

She said, "Not really. Not now. What's your name?"

He tapped her wrist with his forefinger and said solemnly, "Kelvin Walker. Now Jill, will you promise to do me a very great and special favour? One which only you have the power to grant?"

She smiled and said, "If I can."

"Will you take me to the most expensive eating

place in London and will you order for both of us
the most expensive meal on the menu? For which I
will pay?"

She was touched, and said seriously, "That's very
sweet of you, but can you really afford . . .?"

"Tonight there is nothing I cannot afford."

She said, "Well, I can't take you to the *most* expensive restaurant, but I will take you to a *pretty* expensive restaurant, if you're really keen."

He paid the waitress and they went into the street.
He said, "You must tell me if I do anything wrong.
My manners are clean, but not very polished
yet."

She told him just to act naturally.

2
A MEAL WITH
A NATIVE

They ate in a revolving restaurant on top of the
tallest building in Britain. Through wide plate-glass
windows a vision of city roofs and the sky over them
swung continually sideways, the sky lucid and cloud-
flecked and divided by dark, towering office blocks
into panels of increasingly beautiful sunset colour:
yellow-orange in the west, blue-green pricked by a
star or two in the east. Gradually the sky dimmed
and the city itself began shining. Among rooftops
between the offices a glow of floodlights showed the
position of St Paul's Cathedral, Westminster Abbey,
Buckingham Palace. The warm air was filled with
music of a Viennese flavour. Kelvin and Jill faced
each other across a damask-covered table-top. The
waiter had removed the remains of the meal and
they were inhaling, not too deeply, the cigars Jill
had ordered, while occasionally sipping their wine.

At precisely this moment Kelvin attained the confidence to glance casually over the other company in
the room. Though he did not doubt the suitability
of his brown Harris-tweed plus-fours or Jill's shirt
and jeans he could see the others were conspicuously
well-dressed. He waved his cigar toward them and
said, "Is anyone in that lot important?"

Jill said, "The man who nodded to me when we
came in is Caradoc Smith."

"Caradoc Smith?"

"The actor. He's quite famous."

"Famous people aren't important."

"Would you mind explaining that?"

"Not at all. Important people own and control
things, but the public hardly ever know who they
are. Famous people are mentioned a lot in the newspapers, actors and writers and royalty are famous,
but they aren't important."

Jill said, "What about politicians? You read about
them in the papers."

"Perhaps one or two prime ministers have been important," said Kelvin, unwillingly, "though I cannot
at present recall their names. Most politicians are just
rank and file, no matter how much publicity they get."

"What about scientists?"

"Tools, just tools. Tools of the businessmen and
politicians. An employee cannot be important in the
Nietzschean sense of the word."

"What about Jesus?"

He sat up suddenly as if electrocuted and asked if
she was a Catholic.

"No. Why?"

He relaxed, relieved, and explained that in Scotland
only Catholics and children referred to Christ in
that familiar way. She said, "Call him what you like,
but surely you admit *he* was important?"

"I cannot admit that. He had a chance of importance
when the Devil offered to make him king of all the
nations of the world but he refused, I think
unwisely. He would have been a decent king. He
could have introduced reforms and done a lot of
good. But no, he refused the offer and left the

world to folk like Nero and Attila and Napoleon and Hitler. Of course, he became famous and got a lot of publicity for his ideas, but who cares for his ideas nowadays? What important men have ever lived by them?"

Jill said, "What about that German you're so keen on?"

"Nietzsche?"

"Was he important?"

"Not while he lived!" cried Kelvin harshly, "While he lived he was a voice crying in the wilderness. He thought great thoughts. He uttered them. He brought them to no practical outcome. He went mad, and died. But now he is important! Not the old neglected Nietzsche who died insane, but the new and effective Nietzsche who will triumph through me!"

His voice had grown very loud. At nearby tables people sat in the rigid cowed postures the British adopt when something embarrassing is happening. The waiters stared openly. Kelvin beckoned the nearest and in quiet voice asked for the young lady to be given another bottle of what she had ordered the first time. The waiter withdrew. Kelvin saw that Jill had bent her face towards the tablecloth and covered her mouth with her hand. Her shoulders were shaking. He said, "I see I amuse you."

She grinned at him openly saying, "I'm sorry but you strike me as absolutely mad."

"You are mistaken."

"Oh fuck. Have I hurt your feelings again?"

He winced at the oath but said dryly, "Not at all. This situation holds no novelty for me. At the Glaik Free Institute Literary and Debating Society we have some women members and more than once,

in a crowd you know, I've found myself in the café
over the road talking to one of them. Talking, you
understand, mainly for pleasure, but nonetheless
exchanging important ideas. The woman talks back,
she seems to like me, there is an atmosphere of
friendship and gaiety, I feel we are building a kind
of bridge. Suddenly she says something that shows
she is not amused by my words, but by my personality. She regards me as a kind of freak. I had begun
to think things were different in England."

Jill was upset. She said, "Oh don't feel that! Hell,
Jake and I are often called mad too."

The waiter returned, drew the cork and poured a
little into Jill's glass. She tasted it and said it would
do. He filled her glass, then Kelvin's, and withdrew.
Kelvin said suspiciously, "I trust this *is* the dearest
wine on the menu?"

"No, but it happens to be a wine I particularly like.
And it certainly isn't cheap."

"Who taught you about cigars and wine and things
like that? Your boy friend?"

"Jake? God no. He drinks nothing but beer and
smokes nothing but Woodbines, when he can afford
them. Actually, I picked up the bon viveur stuff
from my stepfather. My mother was in hospital
three months with a miscarriage or something and
he took me out to quite a lot of places."

Kelvin, aware of treading delicately, said, "Was this
the stepfather you don't like much?"

"That's the one. Actually I used to like him quite
a lot."

She drank then stared gloomily into her glass for a
while then said, "But he made a pass at me so I
had to leave home."

Kelvin was inexpressibly shocked. He said, 'How horrible for your mother!"
"She doesn't know."
"Didn't you tell her?"
She became exasperated: "How could I? She loved the bastard."
Tears came to Kelvin's eyes. He leaned over the table, grasped Jill's free hand in both of his and cried with heartfelt emotion, "I think we should get married!"

She put her wine-glass down abruptly, spilling some. She heard him say in a quick, quiet, urgent but wholly sober voice, "I have no work or home yet but in a fortnight I will have both. I won't insult you by talking about money but I can honestly promise I possess all the qualities essential to a secure and happy married life."
She freed her hand and beckoned a waiter, murmuring inattentively, "What qualities are those?"
"Energy, intelligence and integrity."
"Sounds like the motto of an insurance company. Waiter, the bill, please." She told Kelvin, "Time I went home."
He glared at the wine bottle. It was still half-full. Grabbing the neck he filled his glass, drank, filled and drank till the bottle was empty. Jill rested her chin on her fist and stared moodily at the ceiling. He put down the final glass and said defiantly: "I apologize."
"Don't."
"I was overcome by drink and sympathy."
"I noticed that. Still, I enjoyed the meal and your company, most of the time. Thank you."
He cheered up at once.
"No, no! It is for me to be grateful. I could never

have ordered such a meal by myself. My first
evening in London has been both entertaining and
instructive."

The waiter gave the bill to Jill who passed it to
Kelvin. He took it in one hand while drawing out
his wallet with the other, but as his eye took in the
price he pressed his lips together, shoved the wallet
back and said to the waiter, "Will you leave us a
moment?"
The waiter left. Kelvin read the bill carefully saying,
"I have no wish to doubt anyone's honesty, but I
am going to be obliged to challenge this."
"But you asked me to order the most expensive meal
possible!"
"I asked you to do that and I meant you to do that,
but 26 pounds 14 shillings and 6 pence is far beyond
the bounds of possibility. They have charged us
seven pounds fifteen for the oysters!"
"They would charge anyone that who had as many
as we did."
"In that case—" he said violently, then continued on
a formal note, "I'm very glad to have met you. I
have now a final favour to ask. I wish to enjoy a
coffee, quietly, by myself. Please leave me here."
She stared at him in horror.
"You mean you can't pay?"
"That is my concern. Goodbye."
"But I thought you were rich!"
"I thought so too but riches, it seems, are compara-
tive. Waiter!"
The waiter came over. Kelvin began saying he was
going to be honest with him but Jill drowned this
with a demand for another two black coffees, then bit
her thumbnail, thinking furiously. Kelvin addressed

her in an angry near-whisper.

"I told you to leave."

"Shut up and let me think."

"My conscience is clear. I will simply explain the circumstances to the management and the mistake which produced them. I've done nothing criminal. I *refuse* to feel guilty about this."

"For Christ's sake shut your bloody mouth. Things are bad enough without you getting pompous about them."

Kelvin raised his clenched right fist toward her, one forefinger didactically extended, his mouth wrathfully open, but when she asked how much money he had he subsided and said coldly, "Twenty-four pounds."

"We need to borrow three. Caradoc Smith might lend that, he used to be keen on my mother. If he won't I'll have to 'phone somebody and get them to come over with it."

She got up saying, "For God's sake try to look casual," and went off between the tables. For a while he sat with folded arms and concentrated frown then took newspapers and notebook out and resumed the copying of addresses. The waiter brought coffees. Kelvin said sternly, "Add the cost to the bill. I will pay you when the young lady returns. Not before."

Jill returned and dropped a ball of crumpled money before him. He took a slim wad of notes from his wallet and settled the bill saying, "I will trouble you for a receipt and the exact change." He did not tip. Jill waited with a set, expressionless look on her face. He said, "Jill! I'm going to repay this money much sooner than you think."

She seemed not to hear.

They went down in the lift without exchanging words or glances. Only the fact that they stood side by side connected them. They moved together through the entrance hall into the heavy, warm, traffic-humming night air where a shared uncertainty made them stop and look at each other. Kelvin said defiantly, "I repeat: this money will be repaid sooner than you expect."

"And where are you going to sleep tonight?"

"I understand that the police do not molest people found resting on benches on the banks of the Thames."

Jill said wearily, "Alright, alright. Come home with me. Jake will put you up."

She walked away then turned and looked back to where he stood frowning at the pavement. She shouted, "Come *on*, Kelvin!"

He joined her saying sullenly, "I would feel happier to accept your offer if I did not feel a certain contempt in your manner of bestowing it."

"Look, I feel a bit drunk and a bit disgusted with myself, see? I don't enjoy borrowing money from my mother's friends."

In the entrance hall of the Underground she asked in a worried voice, "How much have you left?"

He searched his pockets and found six and tuppence. She smiled faintly and said, "I nearly died when you asked for change but I'm glad now."

"There is no virtue in extravagance, as I know to my cost."

"Are you blaming *me* for what happened? Because if you are . . ."

She stopped for he had gone very pale and she sensed he was holding himself upright with difficulty. She took his suitcase, grasped his elbow and moved him with gentle firmness to the ticket desk saying, "You shouldn't have emptied that last bottle."

"There is no virtue in extravagance."

"Do you think you're going to be sick?"

"My punishment is *not* more than I can bear."

The descent into the Underground dismayed him. The forty-five degree slope of the multiple escalators beneath escalators, the lascivious assaults of the Nelbarden Swimwear advertisements, the crowds spilling through gullet-like corridors, the draughts and rumblings buffeting him unexpectedly from strange circular openings were nightmarishly forced into a mind confused by exhaustion, novelty and wine. The one comfortable thing he knew was the guiding warmth of Jill's hand and he concentrated on it, trying to shut out everything else. He succeeded so well that when they sat down in the train he fell asleep against her. She sat with arms folded, his head lolling on her shoulder, receiving glances from the other passengers with an indifference more real than assumed. She cared very little about the opinions of people she did not know and like.

3
THE BASE CAMP

When she shook him awake twenty minutes later he was fit to walk and to insist on carrying the suitcase. They emerged from the station and passed along several dark streets. Jill said suddenly, "Here we are," and led him up a steep flight of steps to a paint-blistered door. This opened into a narrow hallway, feebly lit and papered with a pattern of khaki flowers on a chocolate ground. They climbed two flights of carpetless stairs to a landing where Jill opened a door and stepped through into darkness saying, "Wait."

After a moment Kelvin stepped onto the triangle of light which stuck into the darkness from the landing. He heard faint stirrings, the noise of a struck match, then he saw Jill apply the sudden flame to the wick of an oil-lamp on the draining-board of a sink. She fixed the glass funnel and turned up the wick saying, "The electricity is worked by slot-meter. This is cheaper. Would you shut the door?"

The room was not big but the low light cast large shadows which made it seem so. Kelvin saw a table with a primus stove on it, dirty kitchenware, egg-shells, a nylon stocking, food tins (mostly empty) and paperback novels with lurid covers. Another bigger table upheld a mattress heaped with bedclothes, garments, towels and toilet articles. Between the tables and walls stood a painter's apparatus among dilapidated furniture. Kelvin noticed an easel with a canvas covered with black ferocious marks. The walls were crudely whitewashed and painted with slogans in slanting black print: STOP BEFORE YOU THINK, and HE WHO ACTS IS LOST, and CONSIDER THE LILIES, and GOD = LOVE = MONEY = SHIT. Kelvin read these carefully before seeing a pair of pictures pinned to the wall above the fireplace. One showed a strong old man on a flying mattress extending a hand to touch the finger of a strong young naked man on a hillside. One showed a slim blonde naked woman floating on a big seashell. Jill placed the lamp on the mantelpiece and the pictures glowed like two windows into a more lucid and lovely world. She placed a second lamp on the big table beside the heap of clothing on the mattress and said: "I don't know how you do it."

There was a muffled murmur. She said, "You can sleep forever."

At one end of the clothing heap a hole opened containing a strong alert face. The face said, "Time?"

"Nearly eleven."

Finding himself near a stranger Kelvin jerked erect and stared straight ahead. Jake looked at him and said, "Do I know him?"

Jill said, "No. He's a wee Scotch laddie just arrived in London to take us all over. He's got no money, no friends, and nowhere to stay."

"Is he hungry too?"

"No, we've both eaten rather well."

"I wish I had," said Jake, staring at her. She shrugged and went to the table with the primus on it and began opening a tin. After regarding Kelvin for a second or two Jake said, "Why don't you sit down? Relax. Take off your ... hat."

There was an armchair by the table, its seat covered with newspapers. Kelvin sat cautiously on the edge and placed hat and suitcase on the floor. He cleared his throat and began talking with careful formality.

"Thank you. I would like to start by saying how honoured I feel to be addressing you on my first night in London."

"Why?"

"It seems an honest, respectful way to start."

"Why feel honoured?"

"Because you are the first artist I've ever met. Now at once you will tell me I know nothing of art, and you are right; but artists belong to intellectual élites. I approve of the intellect. I approve of élites."

Jake thrust a naked arm out of the blankets and propped his head on his hand to see Kelvin more clearly. Kelvin was staring hard at the slogan, GOD = LOVE = MONEY = SHIT. Jake said, "You approve of the intellect *and* elites?"

"I do; therefore I am going to ask a question which I hope you won't regard as impertinent. What does that mean?"

Jake said, "I suppose it's a sort of equation. You'll notice it can be broken into three parts."

"Yes, I see that."

"Which part puzzles you most?"

After reflection Kelvin said, "God equals love."

"That's odd. Most people are puzzled by the love equals money bit."

"Oh, I understand that bit. It's obvious. What we love is what we spend money on, and how we love is shown by how we spend it. If a man spends all his spare cash on clothes and none on books then he loves his appearance completely and learning not at all. Again, a man keeping a mistress need only pay her on a weekly or monthly basis because his love is temporary. But if he marries he promises financial support for as long as he lives. That is true love. Furthermore, without money it's impossible to love anything properly. Or anyone."

Jake sighed and said, "Sometimes I'm afraid you're right. But what do you think of: money equals shit?"

"I have my opinion but it might offend."

"Offend then."

"That sounds like an irreverent jibe from someone without much hope of money."

Jake gave a sharp bark of laughter and lay back with eyes closed and hands clasped behind head.

Jill had placed a pan of soup on the hissing primus and now sat on the edge of the table reading, with pouted underlip, a book with an illustration on the cover of someone firing a gun while jumping through a window. Kelvin pondered the picture on the easel then said, "Might I risk offending you even more?"

Jake opened his eyes.

"Risk away."

Kelvin pointed to the pictures on the wall.

"I cannot understand how a man capable of painting these should waste his time on *that*."

He pointed to the canvas. Jake said without rancour, "The first two are reproductions. The one on the easel is mine."

A sad sincere look came upon Kelvin's face. He leant toward the bed, raising one hand like a clergyman at the bedside of an invalid.

"What can I say? Only that ignorance has betrayed me into insolence. I am deeply sorry."

He shook his head deploringly. Jake said easily, "Don't let it worry you. Most people think my painting a waste of time."

"Tell me, what is your picture about?"

"It's about black and white."

"I *think* I understand."

"I think you're being polite."

Kelvin laughed.

"True! I mean those reproductions have a lot of brown and blue in them, but they're not about brown and blue."

"You're damned right they're not. They're about God creating man and about the birth of Venus, Goddess of love. Michelangelo believed in the reality of God and the beauty of man. Botticelli believed in the reality of love and the beauty of woman. Nowadays nobody with education believes much in anything except what they do for themselves. Personally, the only thing I can show people is the reality of the marks I make on a canvas. So that's what I paint."

Kelvin leant forward, eager and alert. He said, "You don't believe in the reality of God? Does that mean you have no faith in Him at all?"

"I wouldn't go so far as to say that. But I hardly ever think of Him. And I certainly don't believe in religion."

"Would I be wrong in thinking that a common English attitude?"

"It's pretty common. Are things much different in Scotland?"

"I cannot speak for Glasgow and the larger cities but in the town of Glaik where I come from people are mostly for God or against Him."

"Which are you?"

After a pause Kelvin said, "Against. In fact I believe God is dead."

"Didn't Nietzsche say that?"

Kelvin was excited.

"You've read Nietzsche?"

"Christ no. But I've heard people say Nietzsche said that."

Kelvin nodded emphatically.

"He did say that. If he had not said it I would not be here."

At the food table the soup boiled over, extinguished the primus and made a lot of smoke. Jill dropped her book, grabbed the pan, found the handle too hot to hold and dropped it on the floor. Jake sat upright and yelled at her, "For fuck's sake how often have I told you when you're doing something to give it your whole attention! *Your whole attention!*"

Jill took the burned fingers from her mouth and said guiltily, "Sorry!"

"You'd better be!"

Jake glared at her savagely for a few moments while she tried to relight the primus, then sank back on an elbow and said to Kelvin, who was staring in an embarrassed way at his hat, "Women! But what has Nietzsche to do with you coming to London?"

"Everything. Would you forgive me if I gave you a little of my personal history?"
"I'll try to."

"My father is a Christian," said Kelvin abruptly, after sucking his lower lip for a little, "in fact he is more than a Christian. He is a Session Clerk. He is Session Clerk of the John Knox Street Free Seceders Presbyterian Church of Scotland...."
"What is a Session Clerk? A sort of Bishop?"
Kelvin smiled.
"Dear me, no. He's not a clergyman at all. He's chairman of the committee elected by the congregation to correct the minister when his preaching wanders from the true doctrine. Well, from my earliest days it was the custom for my father and five brothers and myself to go down on our knees in the living-room above the shop and pray for twenty or thirty minutes before bed-time."
"What about your mother?"
"She had the misfortune to die when I was about four. Nonetheless I have two or three very favourable memories of her."
"This praying, how did you do it? I'm afraid I know next to nothing about Scottish religion."
"Each night someone would what was called *lead* the prayers by addressing the Almighty aloud while the rest accompanied him in their hearts. Usually my father did it, but when my brothers were studying to become ministers one of them would be allowed a fling."
Jake was interested.
"Were those prayers read from a book?"
Kelvin was scornful.
"Of course not! How can you read a prayer out of

a book? It isn't a formula or a poem. The point I
want to make is this: if you had heard my father or
brothers praying you would have sworn they were
talking to somebody in the room, someone not exactly human who was hanging around just above our
heads and paying very close attention. It's a small
room and I felt overcrowded, for I suspected that
the thing watching us did not like me much. Naturally I said nothing of this. I was at a disadvantage
already, being the youngest and having to leave
school at fifteen to help in the shop. I grew confused
and troubled. I went long, brooding sort of walks
by myself but that didn't help. I could feel that the
thing they prayed to was flapping along in the air
above my head like an invisible vulture. Then one
day it started raining, I sheltered in the public
library, and there discovered..."
Jake said, "Nietzsche?"
"I was not ready for Nietzsche. No, I discovered
the sublime Ingersol."

Jill handed Jake a plate containing two fried eggs,
some bread messily buttered, a salt-cellar and a fork.
She climbed onto the mattress and leant against the
mound of his legs as he began deftly and rapidly to
eat. With the first mouthful he said, "Haven't heard
of Ingersol."
"Colonel Ingersol is an American atheist, unluckily
no longer living. He proved that when my father
prayed he talked to nobody and nobody heard him.
The relief I felt was indescribable. You see, though
I never felt God heard me I always felt he was
around, watching and judging and condemning. It
was like having a father with me wherever I went.
Life was a living Hell. Ingersol freed me of that.

For the first time in my life, I felt *alone*, utterly *alone*. The relief was indescribable,"—he smiled to himself—"but I'm boring you."

Jake said with a full mouth, but sincerely, "No, look, carry on, we're interested."

"I visited the library often. I even joined it and brought books secretly home with me. I discovered Nietzsche. He showed that since there was no longer a God to give shape and purpose to life it was necessary for the few who could face this fact to take the responsibility themselves. So yesterday, without telling a soul, I lifted my savings and came here."

Jake was puzzled. He said, "I feel I've missed something. *Why* did you come here?"

Kelvin was puzzled too. He said, "I've just told you why."

Jill said, "Exactly what are you going to do?"

"First I must find a job. I had meant to get a room and then find a job, but as I've no money I'll need the work first."

Jake said, "You can stay with us if you like."

"That's very kind!"

"Not very. We won't be here more than a few days. The rent is overdue. Unless Jill borrows some money from one of her rich admirers the landlady will throw us out."

Jill sat up angrily, and cried, "I tell you I'm *sick* of borrowing money we can't pay back! *Sick* of it!"

Jake said coldly, "I wasn't hinting. I was stating facts."

He turned to Kelvin and said genially, "What kind of work are you looking for?"

Kelvin brought out his newspaper, unfolded it at the marked page and handed it across. He said, "I'll try for these jobs tomorrow. You'll notice I've underlined none whose head office is not in Central London and none whose starting salary is less than five thousand a year."

Jake glanced down the columns. London University was seeking a head for its Department of Ergonomic Studies. The National Society for the Prevention of Cruelty to Children wanted an organizer for its Public Relations Department. The International Libido Canalization Corporation required a director for its British Stereotype Promotion Branch. Jake looked up.

"You've just told me you left school at fifteen to work in your father's shop!"

"It's the truth."

"What kind of shop is it?"

"A small but remunerative grocery."

"What other work have you done?"

"None. I said goodbye to that shop when I put up the shutters for the last time yesterday afternoon."

"Then what qualifications have you for jobs like these?"

"My will to succeed."

Jake and Jill stared at each other. Kelvin smiled and said, "Do you think I'm mad?"

Jake said, "Mad or incredibly naive."

Jill said, "You can't walk into an important job just like that. You've to start at the bottom of the ladder and work up."

"That's not true!" cried Kelvin vehemently. "Nowadays the ladders are so long that the folk who start at the bottom have to retire before reaching the middle. Nearly all the people at the top started climbing a few rungs under it. Furthermore, the nearer the top you get the less real qualifications matter. It's years since the managing directors of

chemical corporations needed to know much about
chemistry. A minister of transport doesn't bother
with railway timetables. The only qualities needed
in a position of power are total self-confidence and
the ability to see when the folk under you are doing
their jobs, and you can usually see that by the
expression on their faces."

Jake said, "Even so, Kelvin, before they give you a
job you have to be interviewed. To get an interview
you have to write a letter giving qualifications and
experience. No qualifications, no interview; no interview, no job."

Kelvin was silent for a moment then said, "Have
you heard of Hector McKellar?"

"No. Yes. Wait a minute. It's one of those names
you hear sometimes but can never remember why.
He used to be a journalist. Isn't he with the BBC
now?"

Kelvin said, "And he's Secretary of the Duke of
Edinburgh Society for the Preservation of Local
Culture. He's a Glaik man, though he left the place
before I was born. Well, I'm going to take his name
in vain."

"What do you mean?"

Kelvin took back the newspaper and folded it into
his pocket.

"Tomorrow I'm going to telephone these firms telling them I'm Hector McKellar and arranging as
many interviews as possible."

"And when you get the interview?"

"I'll explain my deception and the reasons for it."

"They'll throw you out."

"Usually, yes. And I'll be glad to leave, for a
small-minded and unimaginative employer will be

no use to me at all. But once in a while I'll meet a
man or a committee who will want to know more of
me. It will then be my duty to convince them that
my deception is proof of a degree of intelligence and
energy which they would be foolish not to harness
to their own uses."

Jill took a brush from among the bedclothes and
began stroking her hair with it. Jake scratched his
cheek and said, "Maybe you're not naive at all.
Maybe you're fiendishly cunning."
Both men were looking at Jill. She sat with her legs
curled like a mermaid on a rock, a self-absorbed,
faint smile on her downward-bending face as she
soothed herself with the rhythm of the brushing.
Jake said rapidly, "Jill is too conscious of how pretty
she looks sometimes."
She paused, the smile deepening at the corners of
her mouth, and said, "What?"
"I said I'll take down your knickers and spank you
if you aren't careful."
Kelvin lifted hat and suitcase and stood up, saying,
"You offered accommodation. Could you direct me
to the bed?"

Jake climbed down onto the floor, drawing out a
red blanket which he wound round himself toga-
wise. He pulled from the tangle a sleeping-bag and
velvet cushion, bundled them under an arm and said
threateningly to Jill, "You'd better be here when I
get back."
She put out her tongue at him and resumed brushing. Followed by Kelvin he edged between the easel
and an upright piano. They came to a huge dingy
curtain which Jake pulled aside, uncovering a chaise

longue in the bay of a big window behind it. The
space was lit dimly by a streetlamp on the road
outside. Jake dropped sleeping-bag and cushion on
the chaise longue and said, "There you are."

"Thank you."

Kelvin put his case on a chair, opened it and
brought out clothes hangers, clothes brushes and
shoe brushes wrapped in newspaper, pyjamas and a
good suit of dark cloth. Jake stood with arms folded
on chest and watched with interest while Kelvin
hung the suit methodically on a hanger and hooked
this onto an edge of the window frame. Jake said,
"When are you getting up tomorrow?"

"Five-thirty."

"I'm afraid we haven't a clock."

"Don't apologize. I wake automatically at five-
thirty."

"Why bother? You're not working in a shop tomorrow."

Kelvin shut the case and put it under the chaise
longue then took off coat and jacket and hung them
on the other hanger, talking tonelessly.

"On waking tomorrow I'll locate on a map those
buildings where I'll be seeking interviews and I'll
write in my notebook the quickest ways of reaching
them. This will take nearly two hours. Then I must
find a pawnshop as I need to raise loans on one or
two small objects of value which I happen to have
with me. Then it will be time to telephone to
arrange as many interviews for the coming week as
I can. To get all this done before noon I need to rise
at five-thirty."

He paused, facing Jake blankly. Jake felt slightly
daunted. He said, "The best of British luck! If we
aren't up when you go out you'd better take the

spare key. It's on the mantelpiece. I mean we may be out when you get back—we've been asked to a party."

Kelvin said, "Thank you. Goodnight."

His manner was so coldly vacant that it seemed almost hostile. Jake suddenly felt the situation was amusing. He grinned, patted Kelvin encouragingly on the shoulder and said, "Sleep tight, Kelvin."

"I will. Goodnight."

After Jake retired Kelvin stood in his shirtsleeves gazing at the furniture dividing him from the rest of the room. He heard murmurs, a giggle of laughter, then the light beyond the furniture went out. He pulled the curtain, closing himself within the narrow bay of the window, and stood a while thoughtfully biting his underlip and looking lonely and lost. But it would have been a mistake to pity him, for there was a wide range of emotions he never noticed himself feeling.

4
THE
CLIMB
BEGINS

He woke at five-thirty and sat on the sofa in the light of the drizzling grey sky, a jacket round his shoulders, the sleeping-bag warming his legs, the map and directory and notebook open before him. An hour and fifty minutes later, wearing dark suit, clean collar, shoes thoroughly polished, hat and overcoat carefully brushed, he let himself stealthily from the room and stepped lightly downstairs. There was a coin-operated telephone in the narrow hall. With the help of the trades directory he located a pawnshop in central London, then opened the door and stood for a moment on the front step. The rain had stopped and an odour of dampness came from the pavements. It would be two hours before the shop opened so he walked towards it, steering himself by the distant summit of the Post Office tower. The districts he passed through were not rich enough to excite him at first, being mainly rows of small houses with here and there a shopping centre, factory or recreation ground, but eventually he started crossing streets he had walked along the day before, and so thoroughly had his mind digested them that they now had a homely, familiar appearance.

In the pawnshop he placed upon the counter a small brown paper parcel secured by elastic bands. He unwrapped from it a worn wedding and engagement ring, an old-fashioned gold lady's wristwatch with a chain instead of a strap, and on another silver chain a locket which opened to show the head and shoulders of a sweet-faced girl in a wedding veil smiling timidly at a harsh version of Kelvin with a rose on his lapel. The broker said, "Ten quid the lot."

"Could you raise it to twelve?"

"Sorry. Ten pounds the lot."

Half an hour later Kelvin entered a small private hotel and asked if he could rent for an hour or two a room with a telephone; he was passing through London and had several local calls to make. He was taken to a snug sitting room and a telephone placed on a low table beside an easy chair. Unbuttoning his coat he took out the notebook, opened it, sat down and dialled.

He had chosen Hector McKellar's name because McKellar also came from Glaik, but few other celebrities, even Scottish ones, would have served his purpose so well. McKellar had not come to power by brilliant qualities or surprising achievements. Since arriving in London as a journalist he had managed a number of increasingly important jobs in a manner which attracted neither criticism nor praise. He was dependable and dull, but not outstandingly dull, and if this is not the quickest way to advancement it is the surest. His appointment as Director of Britain's least glamorous television programme had not stopped his name being what Jake called "one of those you keep hearing but can never remember why"; nonetheless it was a

name which carried weight in certain quarters. The
secretaries Kelvin gave it to either put him through
at once to their employers or became slightly flus-
tered and explained that Mr Compson was in New
York just now—should they try to contact him? The
employers were affable and accommodating. Three
invited him to discuss the matter over lunch in some
restaurant or club. He replied that at the moment
he was only prepared to discuss the matter in conditions of strictest privacy. Several conveyed tactful
surprise that he should seek a post which was "outside your normal line of business" or which would
be a "comedown from what you're doing now." To
these he said, "I think when we meet I'll be able to
undeceive you on *that* point."
One of them called him by his first name and he
responded with more genial inflections than normal.
The speaker seemed not to notice anything unusual.
On putting the receiver down eighty minutes later
he had arranged two interviews for that afternoon,
five for the following day and six for the day after.
He went out into the hotel foyer in an elated mood
which was damaged by a request for two pounds ten
for the rent of the room and telephone expenses.

In the two hours before his interview with Sir
Godfrey Presley of the Libido Canalization Corporation he ate a snack in a cheap restaurant, walked
to Westminster, strolled thoughtfully past parliament's antiquated spires and continued along the
embankment to the darkly gleaming hexagonal
tower of Libido House. The ground floor of this
building was laid out as a garden. Invisible sources
faintly filled the warm air with the music of
Mozart. Kelvin approached a central reception desk

between flowerbeds of such vivid blooms that he thought them plastic. He told a receptionist, "I have an appointment with Sir Godfrey; my name is McKellar."

She said, "Oh yes, Sir Godfrey is expecting you, Mr McKellar."

She lifted a telephone and said, "Reception here. Tell Sir Godfrey Mr McKellar is on the way up."

She led Kelvin down an alley edged with fountains to a door which she unlocked with a tiny key. It slid aside and uncovered a small room furnished with Persian rugs, a settee and three small paintings of fruit by Courbet, Gauguin and Cézanne. "Sir Godfrey's private lift," said the receptionist with an almost flirtatious smile.

"Just so," said Kelvin, stepping in and sitting down.

She closed the door on him. It opened ten seconds later and he looked out across a blue carpet to a desk with a man standing behind it. Kelvin arose and walked towards him.

Sir Godfrey was bald, broad-shouldered and black-moustached. He pointed to an easy chair in front of his desk and said in a curt, grating voice, "Hello, McKellar. Take a pew," then stared hard at Kelvin and sank slowly into his chair with a puzzled frown. Kelvin sat in a relaxed but tidy posture and at once began to speak quickly and clearly.

"Sir Godfrey, I want to begin by being totally frank with you. I am not Hector McKellar. I deceived you in order to obtain this interview, for though my qualities eminently equip me for head of your Stereotype Promotions Department my qualifications and experience do not. You will see then that as it

is in your interest as well as mine that you employ
me, the fraud whereby I sit here talking to you is
morally justified. The end justifies the means. You
are a businessman so I need say no more on the
subject. But before applying ourselves to the process
of question and answer, challenge and response
which will constitute the main body of this interview
I think it wise to clear one other irrelevancy from
our minds. You have no doubt noticed a stain on
my trouser leg above the right knee—" he tapped it
with his forefinger—"caused by *mince*. On my way
here I visited a self-service restaurant for a snack. It
was an overcrowded place where the customers sat
on awkward stools and ate from narrow shelves fixed
to the wall. Through no fault of mine the mince fell
on my knee from a neighbour's fork. But—" here
he became genial—"explanations of this sort must
seem like swatting midges to a man with your
breadth of vision. You yourself, I notice, have a
small but perceptible egg-stain on your tie. Don't
you feel this makes for some sort of bond between
us?"

During this speech no flicker of expression had
touched Sir Godfrey's louring features. Now he
leant forward and touched a switch on his desk-top
and stood up. Kelvin stood up. A door opened behind him and Sir Godfrey said loudly, "Show this
... gentleman out!"

Kelvin turned and walked towards a doorway with
a young woman in it. Before going through he
stopped and looked back saying, "Sir Godfrey! It is
good that we discovered so soon how impossible it
would be to work together. I want you to remember
this afternoon. A moment ago I called you a man of
vision. I no longer believe that. In less than a month

you will realize how short-sighted you really are. Good-day!"

He closed the door firmly behind him, taking care not to slam it, for that would have been a sign of weakness, then followed the secretary across a room of staring typists. She herself gave him some curious glances he was too preoccupied to notice. Considered purely as a first interview things had gone well. He had spoken clearly and forcefully and kept his confidence throughout, and his one mistake had been the reference to the food stains; it would have been wiser to conclude by saying, "And now what questions would you like to ask?" He would do that next time. He was also pleased by the speed of the interview. If all unsuccessful interviews took so little time he could get through ten or twelve of them a day. He went down in a lift which stopped at many intermediate floors and on leaving it was forced to avoid two official looking men in dark suits by dodging to an exit through a grove of dwarf cypresses and then running like the wind. He decided he would avoid, in future, creating resentment with self-expressive but unnecessary final remarks.

The next interview passed more pleasantly. When Kelvin stopped speaking the man behind the desk laughed heartily and said,"You know, you'll get into serious trouble if you carry on like this. And you haven't a hope in hell of getting a job."
"I prefer to assume that the chances against me are a hundred to one. I shall not start to despair before I have been rejected ninety-nine times."
"Goodbye. I'll be sorry if they jail you."
Kelvin smiled gravely and stood up, saying, "You

are more humane than the last man I spoke to, but not more enlightened."

He spent the rest of the day in a public reading room searching through periodicals for jobs, and after filling seven pages of the notebook with addresses he bought a bar of chocolate and walked back, eating it, to the studio.

He entered as dusk fell, carefully removed his clothes and lay down in the sleeping-bag. His limbs ached with tiredness but his brain was wildly and uselessly lively and repeatedly reviewed the events of the day. "If Jill was here," he thought, "I would tell her all I had done and then I could sleep." He suddenly felt so angry with Jill for being absent that sleep was impossible. He got up, put a coin in the meter and switched on the light. The muddle and squalor of the room leapt so vividly to his eyes that he stood with hands over them feeling he might go mad, then he put on his old suit, rolled up his sleeves, tied an apron on and began cleaning. He swept and dumped all dirt and rubbish into the hearth and burned what was burnable; he collected all books onto the mantelpiece, all clothing into a wardrobe, all canvasses into a corner, all crockery and cutlery into the sink; he moved useful furniture into the half of the room near the door and studio apparatus and ornamental objects into the half near the window. Then he spent time and care arranging all with the greatest neatness, creating where possible an effect of symmetry. A sofa at right angles to the wall on one side of the fireplace was confronted and balanced by a row of three wooden chairs on the other. The food table and bed table were left in the centre of the room but separated by a draught screen. Only the chaise longue was exactly where it had been. After this he washed and dried dishes and cutlery and placed them round the primus on the food table, then stopped and regarded what he had done. The room had an aspect of clinical and rigorous order which made Kelvin now feel thoroughly at home. To the grateful imaginary figures of Jill and Jake he murmured aloud, "Please regard this as part payment for your hospitality. I liked doing it. Man's noblest activity is creating order from chaos." Taking an old pillowcase he began carefully dusting.

He was at work on the big table when he grew conscious of an approaching sound, "Hee-haw, hee-haw," with an undertone of gabble. This grew loud. The door banged open. Jill came in talking wildly, followed by Jake who was drowning her voice by bellowing, again and again, "All right! All right! All right!"
Both fell silent at the sight of the reformed room and of Kelvin whose existence they had completely forgotten. Jill strode to the sofa and sat down saying, "But what I can't understand is you pretending not to like her in the first place. I mean if you think it means nothing why pretend anything? I'd just like to know. Out of curiosity."
She spoke gazing straight ahead with her hands pressed between her knees. Jake lolled against the mantelpiece, watching her grimly. Kelvin, finding himself between them, moved awkwardly across to the sink. Jake said, "Have you finished? Or would you like to add anything?"
She stared miserably at the chairs facing her. Jake said in a hard bullying voice, "Look, if you want excuses you're going to be disappointed. By sheer

accident I was sitting beside her on the floor. I was
a bit drunk, so was she, we all were. Suddenly she
throws her arms round my neck and looks up at me
wanting to be kissed. All right, she's a tart, but she's
an attractive tart, I felt like kissing her and I did.
There's no need to build anything on it, for Christ's
sake I'm not in love with her! When I said I didn't
like her I was telling the complete truth. Five minutes of her conversation would drive me up the
bloody wall."

"But you could neck with her for twenty minutes.
With me there. In a room full of people who know
us."

"Look, Jill, you'd better be careful! I warn you,
you're beginning to make me feel trapped! I thought
there was a decent relationship between us, both of
us doing what we felt like doing and going our own
way when we wanted different things. Carry on like
this and you'll make me feel trapped. I couldn't
stand you then."

Jill frowned slowly and spoke like a child repeating
a new and difficult lesson. "If I'm not careful ...
you won't be able to stand me. I've got to be more
careful in future. I see."

Jake strolled over to Kelvin and said with over-
stressed geniality, "How did you get on?"

"Very well. . . ."

A lamp struck the wall between them and bounced
into the sink sprinkling Jake's shoulder with glass
from the shattered funnel. He brushed it off with
his fingertips saying, "You don't mean you got a
job?"

Kelvin glanced uneasily at Jill who stood on the
hearthrug with feet apart, crouching and glaring.

He said, "No, but I had two interviews and have
arranged eleven."

Jill grabbed a breadknife from the table, raised it to
the painting on the easel and stared across at Jake
who said, "That's very good. Did any of them listen
after you'd told them who you really were?"

"Yes, but not for long."

Jill slashed the canvas diagonally. Jake said, "And
no one sent for the police?"

Jill dropped the knife, seized the floor brush and
swung it overthrowing easel and draught screen,
clearing mantelpiece and food table, then she shoved
the table which ran on castors collecting before it a
mound of furniture and rubble. Kelvin gazed
open-mouthed at the gathering wreckage. Jake
shouted to him over the noise, "Decent of you to
tidy the place up!"

Jill rushed over clawing at his face and crying in a
hysterical whisper, "Bastard! Rotten bastard!"

He caught her easily by a wrist and spun her round
so that she was bent double by the arm twisted behind her back. He took a handful of her thick hair
and tugged. She grunted. He said, "Call me master!" and tugged harder. She made a noise between
grunt and sob, he said, "Call me master!" and
tugged harder still. She screamed, "Master!"

He let her go then and leaned casually against the
draining board with folded arms. She stood and
faced him calmly, terribly pale and rubbing her
twisted elbow. Kelvin stared at them and said in
an aghast voice, "That was a very wrong thing to
do!"

Jake said, "I'm sure Jill agrees with you."

Jill smiled contemptuously and said, "You filthy
exhibitionist!"

Jake nodded gloomily. She stepped neatly to the
fireplace across the intervening mess, picked a
thriller from the heap on the hearth, sat on the sofa
with legs crossed and started reading.

Kelvin, who had witnessed more emotions in
three minutes than he had seen in his whole previ-
ous lifetime, stood half stunned for a while. With an
effort he noticed that Jake was gripping his elbow
and murmuring with a sort of quiet urgency, "I
can't do anything with her when she's in this mood.
Go and talk to her. Cheer her up. I'm sure you can."
Kelvin nodded blankly. Jake went to the studio
end of the room and started deftly and silently
tidying up. Kelvin came to the sofa and sat on it
as far from Jill as possible. She ignored him. He
placed three pound notes in the space between them
and cleared his throat. She said coldly, "Yes?"
"Here is the money you borrowed from the actor
last night."
"You said you had no money."
"Nor had I, but I had a few trinkets belonging to
my mother and this morning I pawned them."
"Oh."
After a pause she added, "You shouldn't have done
that."
"But I needed money myself. And I'll redeem them
in a week or two."
"Good."
She turned a page. Kelvin cleared his throat and
said, "Did you mind my tidying the room?"
"Not a bit."
After a moment she said bitterly, still pretending to
read, "I used to tidy it myself before Jake made it
clear he didn't give a damn what I did."

Kelvin said sympathetically, "Yes, it's hard to do a thing if nobody appreciates it. I did this tonight because I hoped it would please you. Since it does it will be easy to go on doing it. While I'm here, that is."
Slowly Jill let her book drop and turned to face him. From behind them came the discreet sounds of Jake's activity. She said in a low, tense voice, "You like me, do you?"
Kelvin nodded. She moistened her lips and leaned forward, offering her face. He smiled sadly and shook his head. She took one of his hands in hers and whispered, "Kiss me! Kiss me!"
"No. You want to hurt him,—" he nodded towards Jake, "—it won't hurt him because it won't mean anything and I'll want it to mean something."
Jill suddenly sobbed into her hands. Kelvin put his arms round her and said in a reflective, almost musical voice, "I don't know much about love because I'm bad at it but it seems an unnatural emotion. The only people able to comfort us bring us pain. Love should not be like that. Life is sore enough already. Love should simplify and tidy, not complicate and destroy, and does it not sometimes do that?"
Jill clung to him, sobbing deeply. His heart beat so hard that he had to breathe deeply before continuing his thought. He said, "For most people love leads to marriage, and a home, and a breakfast recess off the kitchen, and contemporary wallpaper, and a television set; but somehow that seems ... un-Nietzschean. 'Live dangerously' says Nietzsche. When love stops being dangerous and confusing and no longer needs courage perhaps it becomes something else. Aye, you are right to love him and not me."
Jill became still and quiet, her face resting against

his chest. He patted her shoulder affectionately and said, "Life with Jake is an adventure, dangerous but grand. Tomorrow or the day after the landlord may throw you out. Where will you go then? You don't know but you have friends, you'll find a place. Where will you live a year from now, what furniture will you have, what clothes will you wear? Neither of you know. With me all that would be known, fixed, foreseen. My future is certain because I live by will, not emotions. There must be many like me in London these days, just arrived from abroad or the provinces, outside society but stuck to it by our efforts to climb into the commanding heights. Jake is a true outlaw, a bandit, an ... aristocrat. Not even Nietzsche will save me from becoming middle-class, respectable and dull."

Jill's shoulders shook a little. He said sadly, "Please don't cry."

She sat up grinning and began to tidy her hair saying, "Do you really think it's aristocratic and adventurous painting pictures nobody likes and living by scrounging from your parents and the National Assistance Board, and kissing a prostitute at a party and twisting your mistress's arm when she complains? Don't you think it's rather childish and petty? And do you think it's really dull and respectable to come to London with no friends or qualifications, lose all your money on the first night and then try to bluff your way into a five thousand a year job?"

He looked at her gravely and said, "You should not say these things. They encourage me."

"You're not short of courage."

"Where you're concerned I've none at all."

Jake came to the back of the sofa and leaned over

them saying, "Are you two lovebirds friendly again?
Look, I've a suggestion. It's not midnight yet and
Mike's party will have just started to warm up
nicely. Let's all go back to it."

Jill said to Kelvin,"Would you like to go?"

"No. I've five interviews tomorrow and I need very
regular quantities of sleep."

Jill said, "I'll stay too, I don't feel like a party."

Jake sat on the sofa-back speaking gently and car-
essing the lobe of her ear. He said, "Come off it,
Jill. If Kelvin is going to bed it won't be much fun
sitting reading by the fire, and if you go to bed with
him he won't sleep and you'll spoil his chance of a job.
Besides, you like parties, and this time I'll be a good
boy. That's a promise."

She turned to Kelvin and said almost pleadingly,
"Are you sure you can't come?"

"Thank you: I prefer not to change my mind."

Jake grinned and said, "That puts us in our place.
Come on, Jill, walky-walky."

He pulled her to her feet. She looked into his face and
said, "You think you can do what you like with me."

"Yes. But only because we both like the same
things, though you won't always admit it."

"Take care. One day I may want something you
don't like at all."

Jake took her chin gently between thumb and forefinger saying, "I'll never tie you down, Jill."

For a still moment they stared into each other's eyes.
Kelvin blew his nose harshly and Jake said, "Come
on, it's Kelvin's bed-time."

Jill said, "'Goodnight, Kelvin!"

Kelvin smiled brightly and said, "Goodnight. Have
... fun, both of you."

*

They left, slamming the door. The smile left his face. He surveyed the new order of the room. Jake had only partially restored it. He muttered, "Both of you. Both of you," under his breath but was not thinking about Jake at all. He started tidying up again, moaning savagely between his teeth, "The bitch! The bitch! The bitch!"

5
SETBACK

Next day the earlier interviews wasted very little of Kelvin's time. The alert expectations with which he was greeted became outright rejection in a matter of seconds. But at three-thirty he visited the head-quarters in Whitehall of the Urban Redeployment Commission, was shown into the chairman's office and sensed an unfamiliar atmosphere.

The chairman, Mr Brown, was writing as Kelvin entered and continued to do so. Kelvin sat in the chair before the desk. Eventually Brown uplifted a craggy face and said, "Well?"
He was Scottish.
"Mr Brown," said Kelvin, "I want to begin by being honest with you. I am not Hector McKellar."
"I'm aware of that. Hector McKellar and I were students together at Edinburgh University."
Kelvin was interested. He said, "Why did you allow this interview?"
"Curiosity. I wanted to find why you were taking my friend's name in vain."
"My reasons are basically praiseworthy. You are looking for a Co-ordination Controller for this new

city you are building north of the Wash. I have no
qualifications for the job but my qualities fit me for
it. I had to see you before I can convince you of
this. That is why I used McKellar's name."

"Indeed. Tell me, have you any experience of Local
Government?"

"None."

"Or Civil Service Administration?"

"None."

"Or Company Law?"

"No."

"Have you studied the problems of modern town
planning?"

"Never."

"Have you a degree in sociology?"

"I left school at fifteen to work in a shop. I have not
been to a university."

"Then what qualities can possibly equip you for a
job like this?"

"Energy, intelligence, and integrity."

Brown regarded Kelvin closely and Kelvin stared
calmly back.

"What's your real name?"

"Kelvin Walker."

"You have a high opinion of yourself, Mr Walker."

"I have not tried to hide the fact, Mr Brown."

"True."

Brown leant back and gazed at Kelvin with a
thoughtful frown for a very long time. Kelvin said,
"Would it be impertinent for me to speculate upon
what is passing in your mind just now?"

"No. Go ahead."

"You wonder if I am mad, or naive, or fiendishly
cunning."

"You're right."

"Let me defend my attitude. As Co-ordination Controller I will have departments under me responsible for things like local government administration, town-planning, civil service liaison and so forth. Is that the case?"

"It is."

"The departments will be staffed by qualified specialists who know their work thoroughly. My job will therefore be to make sure they get on with their work and decide disputes arising between different departments. Is this not so?"

"Just so."

"In other words, my success depends on my ability to judge character, to sense the different moods prevailing in groups under my control, and to decide between different courses on a basis, not of specialized prejudice but of sheer common sense. Is this the case?"

"Largely, yes."

"Mr Brown, this is a job I could do and do well!"

Brown sat up stiffly and said, "What reasons have you given me for thinking you have the ability to judge character, sense moods or decide between courses on a basis of common sense?"

"No reasons!" cried Kelvin ardently. "I do not ask to be accepted on reasonable grounds. Reason can only proceed by precedent and I stand before you as naked of past history as Adam before God on the sixth day of creation! I ask to be judged, not by your reason but by your intuition. I appeal not to your logic, but to your courage. Mr Brown, have faith in your heart, which is the divine part of you. Distrust your cowardly brain which can only hobble upon the warped crutches of reason and precedent. Does

not your heart guarantee that anyone who has come
to you as I have come and spoken to you as I have
spoken *must* be fit for this job?"
Brown perhaps felt himself in danger of capitulating
for he reacted violently: "No, Mr Walker, it does
not! I have no wish to be offensive but I suspect I
am facing an abnormally self-assured confidence
trickster with a ... a ... an almost inspirational gift
of the gab."

Kelvin felt he had been struck in the face. His
mouth fell open, he blushed bright red then became
pale and rose to his feet with an expression of horror
and misery. In a feeble, pleading voice he said, "Do
you really think I am that, Mr Brown?"
Brown looked at his blotting pad, slightly ashamed.
He said, "Sit down, Mr Walker. I haven't the fain-
test idea what you are. Inform me, please."
Kelvin sat and in a plaintive monotone gave the
same account of himself as he had given Jake. Brown
said, "Has nobody offered alternative employment?"
"The Kodak Weapons Corporation offered work as
a salesman."
"And you refused?"
"Mr Brown, I have stood for nearly five years behind the counter of a shop and I didn't like it. The
only difference between selling tinned soup to
housewives and missile systems to governments is in
the scale of the material reward and I am not interested in material reward, I am interested in power.
I would rather be on the board of the smallest firm
in London than salesman for the biggest in the
globe."
"You are unrealistic, Mr Walker. Nobody without

money or experience can start straight off at that
level. Even when a managing director is a majority
shareholder it is customary for his son to spend
three or four weeks in some inferior post before
being promoted to the board. I'm friendly with Karl
Dexter of Dexter Delvers. If you'll take my advice
you'll let me speak to him about getting you work
as a sales-representative."
Kelvin said slowly, "If I worked hard at that and
was brilliant at it, what would my prospects be?"
"If you were a genius you might become sales manager in, oh, five or six years."
"And how long will it take a sales manager to become managing director?"
"That is an impossible question. I really can't
answer it."
"And I have no chance at all of this job you are
advertising?"
"None. It concerns a government contract. We are
building this city to rehouse those made homeless
when South London is pulled down under the new
Decentralization Plan. Applicants for the job will go
before a Committee whose members were educated
at Oxford. In the long run they'll employ whoever
I nominate, but only if he seems the sort they'd have
chosen themselves. Frankly I cannot advance your
career without jeopardizing my own."
Kelvin stood up and said, "I will take my leave. I'm
glad to have met you. That reason for not employing
me is the first I have heard with respect."
Brown pushed a writing pad to Kelvin's side of the
desk.
"Give me your address. If I can recommend you to
a position of power without suffering the conse-
quences I'll get in touch. It's hardly likely though."

Kelvin wrote. Brown took back the pad and said,
"One other thing. I positively forbid you to use
Hector's name in this way again."

Kelvin cried out, "Mr Brown! Without that name
I have no plan, no strategy, no reason for being in
London! And I am expected at Transport House in
forty minutes."

"All right, go to Transport House, but it must be
your last interview of this kind. I bear you no ill
will Mr Walker, and this warning is a friendly one:
if I hear you have used Hector's name again I will
tell both him and the police. The business world of
London is large but not as large as you thought."

"And of course," said Kelvin bitterly, "you have
my name and address."

Brown pressed a button on his desk and a secretary
came in. He said, "Miss Waterson, show Mr Walker
to the Executive Lounge and arrange a car to take
him to Transport House."

Kelvin followed the girl in a stunned way to the
door. Brown said, "Remember, I can always get you
work as a sales-representative."

Kelvin turned and said steadily, "I'll see you
damned first."

Brown shrugged and bent over his papers.

Kelvin sat on the back seat of a Mercedes with his
eyes shut, trying hard not to think. Weariness
flooded him. He felt the car stop and heard the
chauffeur say, "Transport House, sir."

Without opening his eyes, he said, "Now take me to
18 Barcelona Terrace, w.c.12."

As he drearily climbed the narrow lodginghouse
stairs he heard from above a loud angry voice which
he assumed at first was Jake and Jill quarrelling

again, but through the open door of the room he saw
that the speaker was a large woman wearing clothes
of a kind which would have looked better on someone younger and slimmer. She was haranguing Jake
who leaned, arms folded, against the mantelpiece,
gravely nodding his head from time to time like
someone receiving weighty information. Jill was
slumped on the sofa in a posture of deep depression.
"Three pounds ain't enough!" the large lady cried,
"just not enough, Mr Whittington. Patient I am
and patient I have been, but a fool I am not and a
fool I will never be. And who are you anyway?"
She was staring at Kelvin. Kelvin said sombrely,
"A friend."
"Yes a friend," said Jake. "Mrs Hendon, meet Mr
Walker, a great patron of the arts. Mr Walker, meet
Mrs Hendon, our esteemed landlady. I'm afraid I
have let her down rather badly, Walker old man.
I'm six pounds behind with the rent. Could you see
your way to helping us out? I mean, you are intend-
ing to buy one of my paintings ... aren't you? Mr
Walker is a buyer for the Scottish National Gallery,
Mrs Hendon."
After a pause Kelvin brought out his wallet, removed six pound notes from it and handed them to
the lady who counted them in a silence broken only
by Jill cursing violently under her breath. Finding
the money correct the landlady said to Kelvin,
"Thank you, sir."
She plainly wanted to say more but found his black
hat, coat and weighty silence so daunting that she
turned back to Jake and spoke with rather less than
her former vehemence. She said, "So far so good,
but this mustn't happen again, see? And another
thing mustn't happen neither. I mean the noise."

Jake was baffled.

"Noise, Mrs Hendon?"

"Sometimes it's parties, but usually it's fighting."

"Fighting, Mrs Hendon?"

"My other tenants are tolerant people, Mr Whittington. They like you and your . . . and the young lady here. But this is the last time I'm warning you. Next time you'll have to leave."

Kelvin crossed to the sofa and sank into it saying, "Mrs Hendon, there is one word which explains all your trouble with our young friends here, and that word is, financial insecurity. When folk are financially insecure they naturally lose their tempers easily. I think you will find that my money will not only pay for the roof over their heads but act as a soothing balm upon their hearts. As Burns once said, 'Art thou troubled? Money will soothe thee.'"

He lay back with his eyes shut and mouth open. Mrs Hendon said, "I only hope Burns was right sir—for everybody's sake."

She went out, resonantly shutting the door.

Jake chuckled, slapped his knees and said, "You're quite an actor! That remote blasé manner is distinctly impressive."

Jill cried out angrily, "And how much money have you now?"

Kelvin opened his eyes.

"Ten shillings. A bit more than ten shillings."

"And how in hell can you live on that?"

Jake said, "Lay off him, Jill. Give him time to recover. I'm sure you're as grateful as I am."

"I'm not grateful. Not at all. That he should spoil his chances to keep us idle absolutely sickens and disgusts me."

Kelvin said tonelessly, "That hasn't ruined my chances. Anyway I'll find work tomorrow."

"How can you be sure?"

"I'll get a job as a bus conductor. Big towns never have enough of them," said Kelvin with a gust of masochism. Jake and Jill stared. He leant his arms on his knees and looked between them at the floor, then shuddered and said, "I've been undermined. A man called Brown undermined me. I don't care that he threatened me with the police and, and, and unless I use McKellar's name what can I do? But he thought I was a confidence trickster and I think maybe he was right. That never occurred to me before! Never occurred to me!"

He covered his face and began crying quietly. Jill laid a hand on his shoulder. Jake started walking up and down the room. He said, "Don't you understand, Kelvin? Haven't you got the point? All these chairmen and directors and governors and politicians, they're all confidence tricksters. Nobody but a fool thinks they're more virtuous than the rest of us, and you've pointed out yourself that they don't even know more. Then why do they get up there? Because most people are so afraid of running their own lives that they feel frightened when there's no-one to bully them. So we get a gang of bullies and tricksters ordering us about and getting very well paid for it. And what makes them so successful? Their confidence. And where do they get it? At home and at school and at university. I know what I'm talking about. My parents are rich. I've been to public school. I'm a member of the ruling classes all right but thank God I'm a decadent member. I'm just not interested in bullying people, except Jill sometimes, when I'm in a bad mood. But you're

different, Kelvin. Nobody has fed you with confidence. God knows where you get it from. And if you
can only kick your way onto the ladder at the very
top rung you'll have shown the whole system to be
as insanely arbitrary as it really is. Which is why
I'm behind you, cheering. You mustn't become a
bus conductor, mate! It wouldn't be right."

Kelvin clenched his fists between his knees to stop
them trembling and turned towards Jill a face so
white and panic-stricken that she leaned towards
him, alarmed. He cried out in a high fast voice,
"I've lost my faith, Jill!"
Jake shouted, "But you don't believe in God!"
Jill said, "In yourself?"
"I've nowhere to go, Jill," he said in a kind of whispered scream. She received his face onto her breasts
and held him tight, then stared sternly over his
shoulder at Jake who was staring blankly back. With
one finger she indicated the door. Jake, worried,
pointed to himself with one hand and to the door
with the other. The look on his face meant: *Me?
Leave? Now?* She nodded vehemently. Gloomily
furious he tiptoed to the chaise longue, bundled the
sleeping-bag under his arm and tiptoed back across
the room. In the doorway he turned and gave her a
long hard stare. She was holding the shuddering
Kelvin in her arms and whispering in his ear. Jake
sighed, shook his head gloomily and went out, shutting the door very carefully behind him.

6
HOLIDAY

Kelvin was wakened next morning by Jill lightly kissing his brow and placing a cup of tea on the table beside him. He lay on the mattress under the heaped clothes with a feeling of almost absolute discontinuity between this particular moment and all that had gone before it. He remembered the interview with Brown, then a period of increasing dread and panic terror, then a chaos of feelings which had turned into unfamiliar exercise. The exercise had involved moments of delight which he could recall only vaguely because he distrusted delight, but he could not doubt the value of the exercise. The sleep following it had been the deepest he had known. Every nerve and muscle in him was enjoying an unfamiliar relaxation. He raised himself on an elbow and said, "How long have we ... How long have I slept?"

"About fourteen hours," she said, sitting on the edge of the table. She was fully clothed.

"That's strange."

"Not really. You've been going at things rather hard since you came here. And then you had something like a nervous breakdown. And I suppose it was the first time you did the other thing."

He looked at her uncertainly.

"Yes. It was."

"Don't you want the tea I made you?"

"Yes. Yes thank you."

He sipped, staring at her across the cup. She said, "How do you feel?"

"Quite well. Very well."

"What are you going to do today?"

After an introspective pause he said, "I have six interviews to attend. I don't care what Brown threatens. I'll go to them."

She smiled and said, "I'm very glad."

He sat up with a delighted grin. He said, "It's queer that something as physical as love can change our feelings about life. I thought only ideas could do that. Jill, only Colonel Ingersol and Frederick Nietzsche have done for me what you have done. Where's Jake?"

"He probably spent the night at Mike's place. I expect he'll be here soon."

"How will we explain it to him?"

"Explain what?"

"The new arrangement."

"Did we arrange something?"

"Won't we have to?"

"Kelvin, I love Jake."

"How can you?"

"He's a decent sort of person."

"I've seen no sign of it."

"I know he acts like a nasty bully sometimes but that's only when he's unhappy. When it comes to sex he's tender, unselfish and rather imaginative. And he loves me."

"Why did he leave last night?"

"I told him to. He wasn't a liar when he said he would never tie me down if I wanted something he didn't want. Anyway, he likes you."

Kelvin frowned and said accusingly, "So we only made love because you pitied me?"

Jill, exasperated, shook her head.

"I wish you didn't put everything into words, it makes them different from how they are. You see I like you an awful lot and I thought you needed me. Look, are you going to get moody about this?"

Kelvin thought for a moment then smiled faintly. He said, "I'm afraid not. I want to get moody about it but I feel too well to be able to. However—" he grabbed her shoulders—"one last kiss, come on, one last precious souvenir of a night of madness, just one."

Jill struggled, giggling, "Stop it, you idiot, let go! Now then, down Fido, down bad dog! Down bad bad doggie. . . ."

Jake came in, the bag under his arm and an envelope in his hand. Jill and Kelvin separated, Kelvin falling back on an elbow, Jill walking to the fireplace where she started tidying her hair. Jake said unpleasantly, "Still at it?"

He shut the door and walked to the sofa, throwing the envelope onto Kelvin's chest as he passed the table. He slumped down with arms and legs spread wide and head flung back, looking very pale. He said to Jill, "How's Florence Nightingale this morning?"

"You've got a hangover, haven't you?"

He pressed a hand to his brow saying, "Oh God, yes."

Kelvin said loudly, "This letter is from the BBC!"

They stared. He read it out.

"Dear   Mr   Walker,

My   good   friend   Mr   Sandy
Brown   recently   gave   me   your   name
and   suggested   that   a   meeting   between   us
might   be   beneficial   to   both.   Kindly
'phone   my   secretary   at   the   above   number
and   arrange   an   appointment.

Yours   faithfully,

Hector   McKellar

PRODUCER OF POWER POINT"

Jill said, "He's found you've been using his name!
Don't answer, Kelvin. It's a trap."
Jake said, "If he was really angry he would have
telephoned the police."
Kelvin twisted a blanket round himself, leapt up,
scooped his clothes from the floor and dressed behind the draught-screen. He said, "I have a feeling
the tide is about to turn. Have you any spare six-
pences?"

He went downstairs to the call-box and 'phoned
the BBC. A secretary said that Mr McKellar could
see him the following morning at ten-thirty. Then
he 'phoned all the other places where he was to have
interviews, giving his name as Inspector McLean of
the Fraud Squad and explaining that a man had just
been arrested for impersonating Hector McKellar
and should not be expected by them. Then he went
upstairs and explained what he had done. Jake, still
slumped on the sofa with eyes shut, said, "I don't
think that was wise."

"Ah, but I have an intuition, a premonition, a conviction that the tide is about to turn."

Jill was frying breakfast over the primus. She said, "It was wise. Kelvin hasn't relaxed since he came here. It's time he saw a few of the sights. Where could we take him, Jake? What would you like to see, Kelvin?"

After a pause, Kelvin said, "I would like to see something of cultural value."

"We could visit the Tate," said Jake. "No, you're a traditionalist. It had better be the National Gallery."

They ate breakfast and set off for the Gallery, Jill keeping beside Jake with her hand under his arm. She was the brightest of the party for Jake had not recovered from his gloom and Kelvin, though seemingly cheerful, avoided looking at the other two. He strolled beside them through the vast rooms with an expression of polite interest sometimes punctuated by pain, for all the nudes reminded him intimately of Jill. Before Tintoretto's "Birth of the Milky Way" he turned impatiently and said, "I am not opposed to art. Please don't think it. But I cannot understand why a vast public building should be given over to decorations more suited to a bedroom or a brothel."

Jake sighed and said to Jill, "Let's take him to the Natural History Museum."

In the Museum Kelvin became alert and lively, taking trips into side galleries away from the other two and rejoining them later with the smiling assurance of a discoverer. In the prehistory section they found him admiring the reconstruction of the

Tyrannosaurus. He said, "The discoveries of science seem to be greatly superior to the products of art. Which of your paintings excel in beauty the corals and conches, butterflies and humming-birds? Or if you think beauty out of date what sculpture could excel this chap for strength and grotesqueness and ferocity? And mind you, he isn't a product of a diseased mind. He was real."

Jake said, "A lot of real things are very nasty indeed. As a whole reality doesn't appeal to me."

Kelvin looked at him alertly and said, "You dislike it?"

"Yes. It keeps hurting me."

"It hurts me too, but only because at present I am a weakling like yourself. If we ever become really strong we will be able to slice off very enjoyable chunks of reality for ourselves. To disparage it just now because we can't do so is nothing but envy and spite."

"What about the millions of weaklings who will never be able to handle reality in the charming way you suggest?"

Kelvin stared into the monster's jaws, his head a little to one side, and said mildly, "I am surprised to hear that *you* dislike the way the strong abuse the weak."

After a second Jake's face flushed red. Jill slipped her arm reassuringly round his waist. He groaned and said, "Oh Kelvin, I'd punch you if I didn't have this bloody headache."

When they left the museum Jake hurried off to his National Assistance Office, for it was payday, and Jill and Kelvin went to wait for him in Ken-

sington Gardens. As they strolled round the pond
Jill said, "I wish you would stop hurting Jake."
"Do I?"
"Almost everything you say hurts him. Don't you
mean it to?"
"Can I hold your hand?"
"Yes, if it won't make you randy."
Kelvin winced and left her hand alone. He stared at
the water and wondered if she would be unhappy if
he drowned himself. Jake came towards them over
the grass, smiling and jaunty. He seized Jill's wrists
and swung her round like a chair on a roundabout
until they both fell down, laughing and dizzy. He
said, "It's amazing how virile new money makes me
feel. Come on, folks, we need food."

As day became evening Kelvin realized glumly
that Jake had no thought of repaying the rent money
though he bought them a meal at a steakhouse then
took them to a pub and ordered pints of beer. He
and Jill met many friends there and introduced them
to Kelvin, who drank heavily but became increasingly reserved. From the pub they went in a car to
somebody's house and drank a lot more in a noisy
overcrowded room. Jake and Jill sat on the floor in
a corner with a bottle of Martini and two glasses
between them. Jake spoke to her in a low voice and
Jill smiled or laughed and stroked his hair. A girl in
a black dress which left her shoulders and most of
her legs bare said to Kelvin, "Hello, are you Jill's
Scotchman?"
"She's a friend of mine."
"Do you paint too?"
He pressed his fists against his chest to counteract

the pressure of anguish inside and said, "I distrust art, I despise parties, and I detest women."

"That sounds quite jolly. I say, are you gay? Shall I introduce you to one or two others?"

Kelvin left the room, crossed a hall and stepped into a cool street under an all but full moon. Taking out the map he located his position and walked back to the studio. It took two and a half hours, and all the way he concentrated on his meeting with McKellar next morning as he had once concentrated on the feel of Jill's hand on his arm.

7
TAKING
THE SUMMIT

In those days the headquarters of the BBC's least interesting television programme were in the premises of a converted cinema in Ealing. The corridors were narrow and dingy. Kelvin was ushered along them into an office that was not at all impressive. McKellar was slow-voiced with vague blue eyes behind thick spectacles. His manner suggested he was sympathetic but found this tiring. He said, "Come in Mr Walker. Sit down. How is Glaik these days?"

"As well as can be expected, Mr McKellar, considering the intelligence of the population."

"I know what you mean. And tell me, how is your father the Precentor?"

"No longer the Precentor. He is Session Clerk."

"Aye, Ramsay Walker was always an ambitious man. Is he on the Town Council still?"

"No, he gave it up two years ago. He thought that the world's business could be more efficiently despatched by agents of the Devil."

"Yes, that view also has much to be said for it. Now then, I wonder what we can do for you?"

"I am seeking work with a starting salary of five thousand a year."

"Perhaps," said McKellar with a touch of asperity,

"I should ask what you can do for us."

"I am in your hands, Mr McKellar. I will try whatever you put me to."

"And you have no qualifications?"

"Quite so. If a clear, quick, vigorous tongue and brain are not qualifications, then I have no qualifications."

"Hm. Sandy Brown thinks your strong suit is personality, and if you have a personality certainly the brain and tongue will be no hindrance. Well, we'll try you with the usual tests."

He lifted a 'phone and asked if studio five was clear, then if Denis Clitheroe was in the building. Then he said, "Well who is in the building? All right, send her up. And lay on a team in studio five, there's a lad coming down."

A blonde woman with a handsome, masklike face arrived and was introduced as Mary Cranmer. McKellar said, "Try him out in studio five Mary. I've arranged a team."

He shook hands with Kelvin and said, "Good luck. You won't see me for a while but I'll be seeing you. Try to act naturally."

The woman led Kelvin along some corridors and up in a lift. She said, "Had any experience of this before? No? Well, not to worry. There's always a beginning."

They entered a dim vast hangarlike space where two easy chairs and a low table looked small and remote in a pool of light in the middle. The woman led Kelvin over to this. A tall bald gaunt greybeard, wearing headphones and a sheepskin waistcoat, came out of the shadows and hung round Kelvin's neck a microphone as slender as a cigarette then directed him to sit down facing the woman. Then the bearded man said to nobody who was visible at first, "OK, Charlie, yes, Charlie. All right Bill, fine, Bill. Ready Hector, certainly, Hector. On you go Mary." The woman told Kelvin, "I want you to suppose I am a Cabinet Minister, say the Minister of Smoke Abatement. On my advice the Government have ordered twenty thousand smoke suppressors at a cost of fifty pounds each for use by the Nationalized Industries, but owing to an error in my office the suppressors are twice the size they should be and virtually useless. Hitherto I have been regarded as a dynamic, popular Minister with considerable prospects, but now the newspapers are raising a bit of a stink. Think about this for a while. When you're ready I want you to ask me questions."

After a few seconds Kelvin said, "Ready."

"Go ahead then."

"Mrs Cranmer, a lot of newspapers are implying that you are a fool. Why do you think that you are not?"

"That is a completely unfair question and I refuse to answer it."

"I'm sorry, I'll phrase it differently. Why do you think the press is being unfair to you?"

"For political reasons. Obviously."

"But surely, Mrs Cranmer, you are a politician?"

Mary Cranmer opened her mouth, hesitated, then shut it again. Kelvin, who had been leaning eagerly forward, leant comfortably back. He knew that in the surrounding shadows and over his head unwieldy machines had been gliding and waltzing, great booms extending and contracting like the necks of dinosaurs, but though tense he was not at all nervous or uncertain. He felt a little as he had

felt in the days when he had believed in God, but it
was pleasanter having his words and actions scanned
by inhuman machinery than by the headmaster of
the universe. The machinery was strictly neutral, it
bore him no ill will whatsoever.

The man with the earphones appeared and said,
"Hector suggests the disaster housewife, Mary."
Mary Cranmer took out a handkerchief, squeezed it
nervously between the palms of her hands and said
to Kelvin in a Lancashire accent, "I'm a housewife
who has seen a jet-liner crash into a row of houses
killing all her neighbours. Think about that for a
moment."
Kelvin said, "I don't need to. What did *you* think,
Mrs Cranmer, when you saw that the plane was
going to destroy all these buildings which were so
familiar to you?"
"I thought, oh dear, the plane's going to crash into
the buildings. And it did! It did!"
"And what did you actually *feel*, Mrs Cranmer?"
"I didn't know what to feel."
"The horror of the catastrophe must have numbed
you to the core," suggested Kelvin.
"Yes it did come as a bit of a shock."
"And what did you actually *do*, Mrs Cranmer?"
"I went and 'phoned me mother."
"Like a frightened child you ran to your earliest
comforter. And then, I hope, you got stuck into a
good meal, something with plenty of meat and po-
tatoes in it. Eating can be a wonderful solace."
"Certainly not!" said Mary Cranmer in her usual
voice.
"Mrs Cranmer, your powers of endurance verge
upon the superhuman," said Kelvin piously.

"Thank you for being so patient with me in your hour of loneliness and desolation."

The man with the earphones broke the ensuing silence.

"Hector says a bishop."

"Ancient or modern?" said Mary.

"Modern of course."

"I am a bishop," said Mary, "who has hit the headlines by consecrating pubs and discotheques and holding communion services in them."

"Why?" said Kelvin severely, "why do you do such things, your Grace?"

"Because Christ should belong to publicans and sinners and *ordinary* people *everywhere*."

"That strikes me as a very condescending remark."

"It was not meant to be!"

"Surely these efforts to court popularity by emphasizing the kindly, everyday aspect of the Christian message are destroying the foundation of it."

"Surely not!"

"Surely yes! Christ's deliberate rudeness to his mother, his vicious flagellation of the moneylenders, his murder of the barren fig-tree all indicate an authoritarian with a touch of sadism to him."

"I disagree," said Mary. "There may be *some* truth in what you say, but—"

"I am attempting to suggest to you," said Kelvin, harshly talking her down, "that intelligent people will respect the church far more if it is less afraid of threatening, denouncing, dictating to, and generally terrorizing us."

"Hector says that will do, Mary," said the man with the earphones. "He says take him over to the staff club."

The McKellar who stood at the bar of the staff club was a more definite person than the one Kelvin had met in the office. He said, "We can use you, Walker. What will you have?"

"Excellent," said Kelvin. "A malt, thank you."

"A gin and bitter lemon thank you, Hector," said Mary. McKellar ordered. Kelvin said, "What wage will I get?"

McKellar was greatly amused. He said, "Heavens, I don't know! I know nothing about finance. What will they pay him, Mary?"

She said, "Well, if he starts with the usual six months' trial period—"

"No no no!" said McKellar, "I want him tied by a firm contract from the very start. I want no repeat of the O'Hooligan catastrophe."

After a pause Mary said, "Then he'll begin at something between five and six thousand a year with six months' salary in lieu of notice if anything goes wrong. If he's any good he'll double that in three or four years. He'll have an expense account for research, wining and dining purposes. And of course the statutory increases to compensate for inflation."

"Does this seem fair to you?" asked McKellar.

"I'm prepared to accept it," said Kelvin. "Will I be handling the sort of folk our friend Mary has just enacted for me?"

"Yes. *Power Point* is the broadest kind of political magazine, we present men who make decisions and the common folk who react to them. At first you'll do Vox Pop—you'll interview people in their streets, homes and factories. Then we'll feed you some backbench M.P.'s, trade-union leaders, Nobel prize-winners and other small fry like that. You have no natural modesty so they'll be no bother to

you. Later we'll throw you bigger fishes—cabinet
ministers, opposition leaders, newspaper pro-
prietors and the occasional ex-viceroy."
Kelvin pursed his lips to stop them twisting into a
small smile and failed. He said, "To be frank with you
Hector, this is happening faster than I expected."

The staff club was a narrow room with the bar
against one long wall and a window overlooking a
dusty yard in the other. Half of it was crowded with
queerly dressed people like the man with the earphones. The half where Kelvin, Mary and McKellar
stood was almost empty. McKellar, glass in hand,
began pacing backwards and forward while talking
in a slightly louder voice. Kelvin and Mary stayed
perched on stools but accompanied him by turning
their faces.
"To be equally frank ... Kelvin ... the BBC just
now is suffering from a dangerous personality de-
ficiency, particularly in the field of regional dialect.
As you perhaps know, the English upper classes
have an educational system which prepares them for
public life by depriving them, during several crucial
years, of all privacy whatsoever. This forces them to
develop an effective public manner and very clear
accents, but it also produces a sameness of tone, and
since nearly all heads of government and law and
industry talk with these tones there is danger that
the ordinary viewer will feel, somehow, excluded.
So what can we communicators do? We can have
them savagely grilled by interviewers with firm regional dialects. The public love it."
"You always call it the British alternative to revo-
lution, Hector," said Mary.
"I always call it the *British* alternative to revolu-

tion," said McKellar, "but unluckily it is becoming
hard to find people who talk their local dialect with
any confidence. I blame the educational system. It
destroys the confidence of ordinary folk and channels the smart ones into universities from which
they emerge as unlike their parents as possible. Am
I right, Mary?"

"Quite right, Hector. My daddy is a Yorkshire
spindle-polisher."

"A month ago," said McKellar, sighing, "the com-
mercial companies had Frisby Mallet and we had
Nick O'Hooligan. But they bribed O'Hooligan away
by giving him a show of his own. We've been looking for someone like you ever since, Kelvin: a
simpleton, but a simpleton who asks, out of sheer
naiveté, all the most pointed and devastating questions. You agree, Mary?"

"I was going to tell him the same thing, Hector, but
less succinctly."

Kelvin stared thoughtfully into his empty glass. He
said, "I think I can play that part with the minimum
of hypocrisy."

McKellar stood suddenly still and pointed an ad-
monitory forefinger.

"Say rather, Kelvin, with the maximum of sincerity!
Hypocrisy is not a word used in television circles.
Sincerity is. Do you ever watch television, by the
way?"

"Never," said Kelvin firmly.

"Then don't. It might destroy your bloom."

Mary said, "Same again, Hector? Kelvin?"

They had the same again. Kelvin said, "I also
would like to buy a round but cannot. The cost of
living in London is higher than I anticipated. Tomorrow I will be compelled by hunger to beg from

a National Assistance office, and I need not tell you, Hector, how disagreeable that prospect is to one of *our* background."

"Surely, in the circumstances, your father will lend you money?"

"I will die before I ask anything from him," said Kelvin coldly. "He opposed my leaving home because he said that without his controlling hand I would reduce myself to penury, crime and the gutter."

McKellar said, "Mary, are you free just now?"

"As free as you want me to be, Hector."

"Good girl Mary. Take him to contracts and have him signed up. Then take him to finance and arrange an advance of two hundred. Will two hundred pounds supply your needs, Kelvin?" said McKellar with a hint of irony.

"I will make it sufficient," said Kelvin, and emptied his glass, and added, "I think I will like working here."

8
SECURING
THE BASE

Some days later Kelvin unlocked the street door, stepped into the lobby and met Mrs Hendon, the landlady, who gave him a glance of immense curiosity. She was obviously going to speak. He prevented this by swiftly lifting his hat to her and saying, "It is time you and I had a talk. May we conduct it in private?"

She said, "Yes all right," and led him downstairs to a half-basement back kitchen furnished as a bedsittingroom. Coals were flickering in a polished firerange.

"Clean and cosy," said Kelvin, "I approve. Now tell me, Mrs Hendon, are you the factor of this property, or do you sublet it, or do you own it?"

"It's all mine, yes. My husband left it me when he departed this life three months last Whitsun. He was quite a bit older than me."

"I am sorry your husband is dead but glad the property is yours. We can talk man-to-man. You notice I am sharing Mr Whittington's apartment. I find it convenient, and I am not a troublesome guest. However, it is only right that you receive a larger rent for the duration of my stay. How much more per week would you expect to get?"

Mrs Hendon bit her lip then said, "Double ... don't you think?"

Kelvin chuckled briefly, produced his wallet, removed some notes and said, "You drive a hard bargain. I respect you for it. Double three a week is six a week, we have three weeks till the end of the month, three sixes are eighteen. Here are eighteen pounds. I am paying on behalf of Mr Whittington also, but kindly make out the receipt to him alone. I will hand it to him myself."

"Yes, if that's what you want."

She wrote a receipt, gave it to him and murmured, "Care to join me in a cuppa?"

"Tea? Why not? Milk and two of sugar please," said Kelvin affably, and sat down.

He enjoyed watching her bustle between sideboard, sink and cooker and was intrigued by the strange little furtive glances she kept darting at him. On a small table she put two pink paper doilies, a plate piled with doughnuts and two mugs of tea. She placed the table against his knees and sat with her own knees pressing the other side of it. He tried not to stare at her splendidly filled sweater and found himself staring at her splendidly filled jeans. She said "Admit it. I saw you on the telly the other night. Go on! Admit it!"

With a pang of annoyance he realized that perhaps she had not been going to order him off her premises. He said stiffly, "That is possible."

"You were asking people what they thought about the South London Demolition Bill. It was wonderful how you got people saying exactly what you wanted without once being bullying or rude."

"When superior politeness cannot get what it wants by superior verbal skill the world will become a jungle, Mrs Hendon, a mere jungle."

"I wish there was more who thought like you, Mr Walker. You know, me mother's mother was Scotch. From Glasgow."

"I hardly know Glasgow but I believe my parents went there on some sort of honeymoon, to visit the British Empire Exhibition of nineteen thirty-eight. We have a tea-caddy at home with a picture on it of the Exhibition Tower."

Mrs Hendon seemed to grow larger.

"Shall I tell you something, Mr Walker? On my grandmother's sideboard we have an exactly similar tea-caddy with an identical picture on it of that self-same Exhibition Tower."

Kelvin smiled and said, "We have more in common than we thought."

"Yes. And now you know what it is."

"Strange how differences of race and religion and philosophy and education and income and outlook can dissolve before the magic of a humble tea-caddy. I notice that you type."

He pointed to a portable machine. She said, "Yes I do a bit of temping, when I can get it."

"Temping," said Kelvin thoughtfully. "A verb made, no doubt, from the adjective *temporary* which is here taken to qualify the unspoken but implied noun *secretary*. I always got top marks in grammar even if I did leave school earlier than a boy should. If I need secretarial help, Mrs Hendon, I will bear you very much in mind."

"*Bare* me, will you? In mind? And very much? Oo! I might like that Mr Walker," giggled Mrs Hendon. Feeling terribly disturbed he quickly drank his tea and said goodbye. Mrs Hendon strongly attracted him but not like Jill did. He felt he had power over Mrs Hendon and none at all over Jill.

He saw little of Jill these days. He still slept on the chaise longue behind the curtains of the bay window, and still got up well before eight to walk to work, not because he wished to save money but because this used up time and energy which would have been otherwise spent in sexual frustration. *Power Point* was broadcast five days a week at ten in the evening, it had a large staff and a lot of shift work, but on his mornings and afternoons off Kelvin, when not shopping, sat in a discreet corner of a studio gallery or cutting room and watched the making of programmes in which he had no part; programmes in which MP's wrangled about the results of earlier wrangles in the House of Commons; programmes in which heads of industry and government minimized their own blunders and each other's achievements; programmes where teams of specialists disagreed about the effects of what had become inevitable. He found this fascinating, but less fascinating than the firm professionalism which turned such crude material into exact scenes in the shadowy opera of the evening's entertainment. He normally left the building around nine, dined at a restaurant, drank a half-pint of bitter and a small whisky in a pub, then walked back to the apartment which he reached in a state of exhaustion sufficient to ensure immediate slumber.

But though his meetings with Jake and Jill were few and brief his presence in the room became increasingly tangible to them. Objects were delivered there in his name: one week a television set, clock and electric cooker; on the next a gramophone, teaset and sofa cushions. As the month advanced the objects became less practical and the studio so cluttered that Jake could no longer stand back from his canvas while painting. His solution was to place pieces of furniture on top of others with Kelvin's highest and out of reach, but Jill objected.

"He's trying to be nice to us. Jake."

"What's nice about turning the room into something like a suburban whore-house? Why can't he be nice somewhere else?"

"I don't like it either."

"Tell him to clear out then and take his junk too."

"You tell him."

Jake lifted a half-completed canvas off the easel and put his foot through it, then hurled it at the end of the room where it crashed into a set of flower-patterned coffee cups on the draining board. Then he went out, slamming the door.

Kelvin came home that afternoon and found Jill sprawling with a book on a new ponyskin rug in front of a new electric fire that looked like smouldering logs. She wore a very short skirt. She said, "Hello! Have they given you the sack?"

"I've the afternoon off because I'm working tonight. I'm giving my first really big interview tonight."

"Who is it with?"

"Dylan Jones."

"They *are* pushing you," said Jill, looking back at her book.

"I wish you were more impressed," said Kelvin, "and I wish you wouldn't lie on the floor like that wearing a skirt like that."

"I'll lie where I like and wear what I damn well please."

Kelvin came near to her, knelt, seized her hand and

pressed it to his chest. He said, "Do you feel something?"

"No."

"That's funny. I feel my heart beating very loud indeed."

"Well, it's your heart."

Kelvin walked moodily round the room. Jill said, "Kelvin, are you honest?"

He went pale, his mouth fell open and his face was twisted by confused emotions. He even stammered slightly.

'Wh-What do you mean, woman? Honest about what?"

"I don't know—about life, I suppose."

He smiled with relief and said, "I won't pretend I have never told a lie but I think where life is concerned I'm more honest than most."

"Then why don't you get a room of your own?"

"Who would pay the rent here?"

"I would. I'm starting work as a waitress tomorrow. It's a job I'm quite good at—I've done it before."

"What's the wage?"

"Five pounds a week plus tips."

He cried contemptuously: "You can't pay the rent out of that."

"Yes I can! And if I can't I don't care! It's not good for us to live like this! Before you came we often managed to pay the rent, Jake had his Assistance money or sold a painting or his father sent a cheque. If one landlord chucked us out we would stay with friends till we found a room elsewhere. We managed. We had to manage. We had a kind of independence. Now we depend on you."

Kelvin said eagerly, "I don't mind!"

"But I mind! And Jake minds!"

"He hasn't told me to leave."
"How can he when he owes you a month's rent?"

Kelvin walked to the sink and stared at the torn canvas and broken cups, then he turned and spoke brutally and desperately: "The reason I don't get another room is that I don't want to leave you. If Jake tells me to leave I'll refuse. If he throws me out I'll get Mrs Hendon to give me a room in the same house. If you shift house I'll hire detectives to find where you live and I'll shift as near as I can. Do you understand?"
"But I don't love you, Kelvin!"
Kelvin stepped quickly over and knelt before her, staring into her eyes. He said, "How can you be sure of that? No, you can't be sure! You're not sure. How can you feel you don't love me when every bit of me is intent on you, intended for you?" (He took her hands in his.) "Jill, don't argue with what I say, just listen to it, and don't listen to the words, listen to the sound. If I am dishonest it's my words that are wrong, not the feelings, so listen to the music of my words, not the meaning. Let my voice be a current joining the sound of my heart to the sound of yours, making it beat the same way."
His voice had grown softly ardent and compelling. She stared into his eyes and said almost inaudibly, "Stop."
"How can you be certain you don't love me? Certainty isn't easy in a world as big and as strange as this one. Listen, I want to leave you and I can't and it's your fault. If you didn't keep me here I would walk out at once, but you keep me here because you need me. You know you keep me here!"

Jill shook her head in a lost frightened way. He said softly, "Yes, you do it. You know you do it. Why do you do it?"

"I ... I'm not sure ..." Then she awoke and jumped up saying, "For Christ's sake, Kelvin, come off it!" He slumped down with his head in his hands, totally defeated.

Jill took a brush from the mantelpiece and stroked her hair hard with it saying, "It's no use, Kelvin. You're here because you want to be here. You can't hypnotize me into believing anything else."

"I'll leave when you want me to."

She saw tears moving down his cheek. She dropped the brush, sat on the sofa and stared at him, open-mouthed and slightly pitying. She said, "Crying?" (He smiled and nodded.) "So you are. But all the tears are coming out of the same eye. How odd."

He said without violence, "I'm sick of my oddity."

"Kelvin, there's no need to be sad. We can still meet each other. And now you know the price of things you can take me for meals you can afford."

"Yes."

"And let's face it, I'm the first girl in London you spoke to. Now you're on television all kinds of gorgeous little popsies will be throwing themselves at your head."

He said dryly, "I wish you'd stop trying to console me. It's condescending of you."

She said more coolly, "I'm sorry."

"When must I leave?"

She put a hand on his shoulder.

"There's no hurry, Kelvin. Don't leave before

you've found a thoroughly nice place where you'll
be really comfortable."
"Thank you."

They were staring at each other sideways in a
puzzled way when Jake returned. He said, "Having
fun?"
"I've been trying to make Jill leave you," said
Kelvin.
"Any luck?"
"None."
"Hard lines."
Kelvin stood up and said, "I'd better go. I'm interviewing the Prime Minister and had better not be
late for the rehearsal."
"You mean those gloriously spontaneous interviews
are rehearsed?"
"Not rehearsed exactly, because when it comes to
the real thing I always ask a few unexpected questions. But people need time to get used to the tele-
vision atmosphere and to start thinking along the
right lines."
Jake said venomously, "I bet you're very good at
getting them thinking along the right lines."
Kelvin seemed pleased and touched. He said, "Yes!
You're right! Have you been watching me?"
Jake went to his easel, set a board on it and started
mixing up on his palette a strong paste of paint. Jill
had resumed reading. Kelvin walked to the door and
said, "Well. Cheerio."
Jill said kindly, "Goodbye, Kelvin."
Jake said nothing. Kelvin left.

For ten minutes after the door closed Jill pretended to read and Jake pretended to paint. In a

pause between two careful strokes he remarked,
"I'm glad Auntie Kelvin remembered to tidy up today.
I was afraid being on the telly would put the good
lady above such things."

"I tidied the place up."

"Why?"

"I've realized I don't enjoy dirt and mess as much
as you made me think. Any objections?"

"Why no! If you enjoy tidying, tidy. I've never been
an enemy to self expression."

He dipped a rag in turpentine and furiously
scrubbed out what he had done, saying, "Be bold,
fearless, free, uninhibited."

He seized a vase of slightly wilting flowers, raised
the rim to his nose, sniffed and said, "I hate to be
critical but this water is starting to stink."

Ten minutes later she said, "How much money have
we left?"

"Twelve bob or so."

"It's not enough, is it?"

Jake seized the rag and again furiously scrubbed out
what he had painted. He said, "What do you want
me to do? Get a job as a bus conductor? And while
we're on the topic why don't *you* get a job?"

"Tomorrow I'm starting as a waitress in the Gay
Hussar."

"Good! Good! So what's the bloody fuss about?"

Jill turned a page and said, "I'm not fussing. Everything's lovely. Kelvin will stop paying for you and
I'll start so everything is lovely."

Jake clenched his fists and said with quiet vehemence, "Christ, this is going to be a good evening.
This looks like being a really lovely evening."

Jill said, "Doesn't it?"

9
THE CONQUEST
OF
LONDON

The magazine programme *Power Point* had been
conceived by a liberal BBC governor whose under-
lings called him The Prevailing Consensus. He regarded it as a public service. "The army exists to
protect us from foreign invasion," he said, "*Power
Point* exists to inform us of our political situation.
Entertainment should not be the primary task of
either—plenty of organizations exist to provide
that."
The first producer he appointed was a non-Marxist
sociologist and free-lance journalist who had written
articles equally denouncing trade union differentials
and British investment in South Africa. This man
said, "*Power Point* will present, without prejudice,
all the political issues which most seriously divide
the country."
He paid spokesmen from the main parties to debate
nuclear armaments, British entry into the European
market, monopolies, social inequalities, local
government corruption, high rise housing, industrial
pollution and Scottish self-government. Since he
was naive enough to believe what he had been
taught at school about the British party system he
found the debates disappointing. He told his chief,

"They don't really disagree about these things—
they just pretend to."

"Which proves the country is not seriously divided," said the governor. "Aren't you glad?"

"But many people believe there are important
abuses which the government ought to tackle. Some
of them *must* notice that the politicians they elect
are not doing that. Perhaps I should give these
people a voice in the programme too."

"No," said the governor, "those you refer to are a
minority when compared with the whole, and *Power
Point* exists to show the political situation *as a whole*.
Since the nation's leaders choose to make politics a
form of shadow-boxing we will falsify the situation
if we show anything else."

"Shadow-boxing makes bloody boring television."

"*Power Point* is a public information service. It does
not need to be interesting," said The Prevailing
Consensus.

But the producer was a romantic who loved excitement. He was visited by a back-bench MP who
told him that the British Gas Board had just discovered an important oil field under British territo-
rial waters. There might be many of these. The MP
thought this was an important discovery because
Britain was moving from a coal to an oil-based economy and the oil legally belonged to the British
people. He wanted the government to promote a
National British oil industry instead of leasing the
oil to international corporations whose main base
was American. The MP was obviously a left-wing
fanatic, but since neither press nor parliament had
yet referred much to the existence of British oil the
producer decided to make a documentary film about

it and show a hard-hitting debate between the back-
bench MP and the presiding minister of fuel and
power. He started arranging this and three days
later had been replaced by Hector McKellar. The
Prevailing Consensus explained that his first producer had failed to grasp the nature of television *as a
medium.*

McKellar knew more about practical politics than
his predecessor, but he too was a romantic who
wanted the programme to be interesting. Since a
clash of significant ideas was regarded as bad television he liked to present, at least once a fortnight,
a clash of personalities. This clash was seldom dis-
cordant but had to be startling. At that time the
most definite personality in British politics was
Dylan Jones, the only trade unionist ever to become
prime minister. His father had owned a small but
profitable business, he was a highly literate man, his
union (The Confederated Precision-Tool-Draughts-
men and Architects) had been the white collar sort,
but his Welsh accent made many working-class
people feel he was one of them and gave his
middle-class supporters feelings of friendly condes-
cension. In the world of BBC television the most
definite personality (in McKellar's opinion) was
Kelvin Walker. He was not yet famous but three
weeks after he joined *Power Point* the viewing
figures had risen by 19.83%. McKellar believed that
a collision between a Scottish and a Welsh accent
would greatly amuse the English viewers and make
his newest employee a national celebrity. He told
Kelvin, "Force the pace of the questioning a little.
Be sharp, but not painfully sharp—he's new to his

job and still popular. Keep your stiffest question till last and make it a personal one."

"Right," said Kelvin.

He felt perfectly at home in studio five that night. He was sitting where he had first sat during the test with Mary Cranmer, and felt that the small, sturdy, balding but professionally relaxed person facing him was a perfect foil to his own urgent leanness. When a red light indicated that the cameras were alive he said, "A thing that puzzles me, Mr Jones, is why you, as leader of Her Majesty's government, pursue a policy of decentralization which you opposed again and again when you were in actual opposition."

Jones nodded and said, "I'm glad you asked me that, Kelvin. There's nothing puzzling about it really. The present government is not opposed to decentralization *as such* but it *is* opposed to unrestricted competitive decentralization. Half the United Kingdom live in obsolete urban conglomerates, the country as a whole suffers from the difficulty and inconvenience this overcrowding causes, and decentralization is the only answer. But this decentralization can only be efficiently and humanely and safely obtained by a government which is not afraid to co-ordinate, co-ordinate, co-ordinate."

The bland exchange of verbal counters proceeded at a brisker pace than had been indicated at rehearsal while the great cameras swung and waltzed above and around, sometimes focusing on a hand or eye or tongue wetting a lip, sometimes zooming back to show Dylan between Kelvin's knees or Kelvin over Dylan's left ear. At length Kelvin saw there were five minutes before the end. He said suddenly, "Mr Jones, you will admit that your programme of combined co-ordination and decentralization involves the biggest expenditure of manpower and money ever mounted by a British government in time of peace. ..."

Jones smiled and shook his head saying, "No. Oh no."

"You don't admit it?"

"No, I don't admit it. I insist on it!"

Kelvin smiled and said, "Nobody will quarrel with you there. But this programme will create innumerable precedents in the fields of local government, company law, civil service administration and modern town planning. Now I wonder if you will let me ask a rather personal question?"

Jones raised his eyebrows and said coolly, "Fire ahead."

"Are you not the only member of your cabinet without a university education?"

"Quite right. I grew up during the black years of the depression. I had to leave school at fifteen to help my father with his milk delivery business. I've not forgotten those years. I don't want to forget them." (Jones stared into the lens of the operating camera.) "Some of those viewing tonight will know what I mean." (He smiled at Kelvin.) "No, I'm not a university man."

"Then what qualifies you to lead a nation at a time like this?"

Jones sucked his pipe thoughtfully and frowned. He said, "You know, we British distrust specialists. Oh yes, we need them, but we need them to do the things they know about and two things a specialist will never understand is how to lead a party and how to govern a nation. These things can only be done well on a sound basis of ordinary down-to-earth common sense. Right? Now if you ask me why my party chose me to lead them, and why the British people elected me to govern, I can honestly say I don't know, but I hope . . ."

He paused and pointed the stem of his pipe at Kelvin's waistcoat. Kelvin said, "Yes?"

"I hope it is because I'm not easily tired by my work and can keep on at it when a lot of others would have to stop. I hope it is because I can tackle a problem on a basis of common sense rather than specialized prejudice. I hope it is because I am not afraid to call a spade—or anything else—by its real name."

Kelvin said, "Or to put it in three words: your qualifications are those of energy, intelligence and integrity."

A wave of delight started to travel across Jones's face but was overtaken and quelled by a wave of caution. He smiled crookedly and said, "You said that. Not me."

"Mr Jones, thank you very much."

The lights went on all over the studio. Kelvin leaned back in his chair and Jones leaned forward to tap out his pipe on the ashtray. Jones said, "That went very well."

"I think so."

"You asked me one or two things I hadn't quite expected, but I weathered them, eh? I weathered them."

"You weathered them"

"New to this game, aren't you?"

Kelvin looked worried. He said, "Was I not professional?"

"Oh yes, you were professional. I just haven't heard your name before."

"I'm new here."

"Where were you before?"

"My father's grocery."

Jones raised his eyebrows. Hector McKellar came in smiling broadly, congratulated them and suggested they come for a drink. Jones said, "Thanks, Hector, I haven't time. I would like, though, a brief word with your young colleague here. In confidence, that is."

McKellar nodded to Kelvin and withdrew.

Jones carefully relit his pipe and said, "Your father's grocery. Why?"

"I had to help him because my elder brothers were studying to be ministers at Strathclyde University."

"What's his religion?"

"United Seceders Free Presbyterian."

"My own folk are Methodist. How did you get a job like this?"

Kelvin told him. Jones pondered then said, "What are your politics?"

"So far I have not had time to consider politics. My preoccupations have been philosophical."

"Nietzsche, I suppose."

Kelvin struggled to hide his surprise. He said, "Nietzsche, yes! Do you read him?"

"I used to but he's a bit too intoxicating for someone setting out into public life. I don't deny his value as a liberator but it would be wiser to get down to something more solid. Read Shaw. He's under-rated nowadays but his political stuff is a useful bridge between Nietzsche and modern political economy. Then I would try Keynes, of course, Winterbeam, Cropford and Mabel Sickert-Newton. But especially Winterbeam."

"I'll remember those names."

"There's a little book I wrote myself some years ago, 'World Order in an Exploding Universe'. It's a bit idealistic but there's some ideas in it you won't come across elsewhere. It's out of print now but if you like I'll send you a copy."

Kelvin brought out a card from his waistcoat pocket and handed it across saying, "My address."

Jones pocketed it. He said, "I'll be frank with you, Kelvin. The party is too full of university men. Our appeal isn't broad enough. You are an unusual phenomenon nowadays, a clever self-educated man who can speak with confidence and conviction. We can use you."

"Shall I join your party?"

"No, not for a while. Take three or four months to get yourself established here, perhaps longer. In the past men rose to fame by their employment of power, but in a television democracy it can work the other way round. Has Haversack been in touch with you yet?"

"Lord Haversack of Ditch?"

"Yes."

"He has not been in touch with me. Why should he be?"

"He likes clever men. I'll drop a line to him. He'll ask you round for dinner one evening."

"I, er, thought," said Kelvin, delicately, "that you and he were opposed to each other. Politically."

Jones chuckled and stood up saying, "Which is one reason why you should not go into politics before we give you the word. You have a great deal to learn, my boy, but you've no dogmas so you'll learn fast. Oh, yes, I can see that."

As they moved toward the door Jones said, "Not married, are you?"

"No, not ... not yet."

"Eye on someone?"

"Yes."

"Is she photogenic?"

"Very."

"Is she respectable?"

"She would be, if she married me."

"Get her to do it. A respectable photogenic wife is an asset, publicity-wise. Do you play golf?"

"No, but – " boldly – "I'm willing to learn!"

"Good. We've too few golfers in the party. A Scotch golf-playing ex-grocery assistant with a photogenic wife and a strong TV personality could be worth jewels to us at the next election. Jewels."

As they separated at the door Kelvin said, "And you'll remember to send that book?"

"Don't worry, I'll keep in touch."

Kelvin left the building feeling like a giant. For the first time in his life he hailed a taxi. He lay in it praying that Jill had seen the programme. He knew she was not as impressed by public success as she ought to be but things had gone so perfectly for him that he felt there was nothing he could not desire and obtain. The taxi seemed less to run through London than soar over it like an eagle. He was amused to notice that without a single lecherous thought he had a pronounced erection. He strode upstairs to the studio so self-obsessed and exultant that it took a while for certain cries to penetrate his mood.

Mrs Hendon stood in the middle of the floor yelling at Jake, "Tonight! You've got to leave tonight!" The studio was covered with an uneven layer of wreckage from which only a few articles of furniture stood out intact. Chairs, television set, electric fire, standard lamp, record player, clock and crockery had been conscientiously shattered and the refrigerator and electric oven were badly bent in the middle. Jill lay on the sofa with her face against the back of it, looking injured. Jake leaned casually against a table with his hands in his pockets saying, "All right. We'll leave tomorrow."

"I said tonight! You leave tonight or I call the police! Come back tomorrow for your stuff, come back with a rubbish cart if you like, but you're not staying another night here and that's flat!"

"Be reasonable, Mrs Hendon."

"You tell me to be reasonable. That's very good. Very good indeed. I'll tell you why I don't want you here tonight. It's the noise, but not just the noise. I don't want murder done on my premises."

Mrs Hendon shook Jill's shoulder gently and said urgently, "Are you all right, dear? A doctor do you want?"

Jill said wearily without turning, "Please leave me alone. Please leave me alone."

Mrs Hendon turned to where Kelvin stood ankle deep in a rubble of paint-tubes, books, food and broken plates. She said, "Well, Mr Walker, you see how matters stand. I gave him fair warning—you'll bear me out—fair warning more than once, but he just doesn't care about others any more than a wild ravening beast. He leaves tonight or I'm getting the police. You can stay, Mr Walker—and the young lady can stay if she likes—I'm not forcing her out—

but you're going Mr Jake Whittington, yes! Or it's
the police!"

She marched to the door where she turned and
shouted, "Not a minute past midnight, see?"

Jake shrugged. Jill turned round and sat up, brushing her hair back with one hand and touching delicately with the other her right cheek which was red
and swollen. Mrs Hendon's mouth and eyes opened
wide. She glared and pointed and yelled at Jake,
"Look at her face you bloody sadist!"

Then she said some more about midnight and the
police and went away.

Jake gazed gloomily at the floor. "I wish the good
Hendon was right, Kelvin," he said. "If I was a
sadist I might get fun out of life. Actually I find it
a continuous wearying effort to make Jill a few
degrees more miserable than she makes me."

Kelvin went over to the sofa saying, "Jill."

She sat sucking her thumb and staring straight
ahead. Kelvin went as near her as he could without
crowding her. Jake found a duffel bag on the floor,
threw it on to a table and started moving around
picking up various articles of clothing, mostly his
own. He said, "It had to happen sometime. We've
been here too long. We've been here far too long.
That's been the trouble. Come on, Jill, pull yourself
together."

Jill stood up, felt dizzy and almost collapsed. Kelvin
steadied her by a hand on her shoulder. She shook
her head, went to the table, placed her hands on it
and leant there, staring down at the bag and articles
Jake kept tossing beside it. Jake was saying, "Well,
Kelvin, it's all yours. A room of your own at last. I
owe you some money, I suppose. Well you can have

the furniture. It's not all damaged. I'm sorry about your television set and refrigerator and so on but hell, we didn't ask you to bring them here. In fact you didn't ask us if you *could* bring them here."

He brought a pile of paint-tubes and brushes to the table saying, "Come on, Jill, get your things."

She turned from the table in a dazed way and bent to lift a crumpled blouse while Jake started packing the kitbag. Kelvin stood with elbows on the mantelpiece and face to the wall and said, "Are you really leaving with him?"

She paused, crouching on her heels. Kelvin said, "I think you should stay here with me. In fact I want you to. I'm asking you to."

Jake grinned and said, "Well, well. I'll say this for Auntie Kelvin, she tries. You've got to hand it to her."

He glanced at Jill and said gently, "Come on, Jill, bring your things here. I'll pack them."

Kelvin said, "Yes, he knows when to be gentle."

Jill paused and Jake yelled at her: "I said bring them over here!"

She flung down the blouse and yelled, "Why the hell should I?"

Looking toward her Jake had a sudden sense of nightmare, for behind her seemed to stand someone he had never imagined in his life, someone whose face was lit by a huge grin of triumphant malignant soundless laughter, a grin too extreme to be human. Jake said shakily, "Look. Look at his face."

Jill glanced toward Kelvin who stared back with straight sad eyes and said gently, "Stay here please. Stay here."

She turned to Jake and said pleadingly, "Jake, let me stay for tonight."

"Stay here with *him*?"

She put her hand to her bruised cheek and cried hysterically, "I don't want to go out tonight! I don't want to see anyone!" and sat on the overturned refrigerator with her face in her hands.

Jake had the uncanny sensation of being part of a world he could not control. Even when smashing furniture in the heat of wrath he had basically been doing what he liked, but now he felt reality was being pulled like a rug from under his feet by forces he could not recognize, though Kelvin, standing still and wooden, seemed to be the centre of them. With an effort he acquired a surface coolness and kept it by continuing to pack the bag. He wrapped the paint-tubes in an old shirt before putting them in, saying, "Please yourself of course. ... Where did I put the ultramarine? ... Yes, Kelvin will be very pleased to have you. I never thought once would be enough for him but I thought it would be enough for you. There's no accounting for tastes. After this I'm finished with you, you understand that, don't you?"

He glanced at her quickly then said, "Socks, brushes, shoes, paint ... ah, my flake white. I can't go without my flake white."

He started hunting round the floor. Kelvin picked up a tube from beside his foot and held it out. Jake came over and paused, staring blankly at Kelvin's blank face, then said, "Thank you," and took the tube back to the table saying cheerfully, "Well, Jill, are you coming?"

She didn't move.

"This is your last chance, Jill."

Kelvin stepped over to the refrigerator and placed his hand lightly on her shoulder. She shook it off. Jake put the tube in the bag, drew the string and knotted it. He said conversationally, "By the way, Kelvin, there are one or two things you ought to know about her. We've not been the only fishes in her little sea. Ask her about her stepfather sometime."

Jill jerked her head erect and shouted, "Shut up!"

"It's an interesting story. . . ."

They raised their voices to shout each other down, Jill crying "Shut up! Don't," then "Please shut up!" "Please, please don't!" Then she burst into tears and Kelvin held her and she clung to him. Jake was saying, "Yes! While her mother was in hospital she slept with him, a man supposed to be her father. No wonder she's ashamed to meet her mother. Did you know she's too ashamed now even to open her letters?"

The silence which followed, though broken by Jill's sobbing, sounded unusually final. Kelvin said, "I think you may leave now."

Jake's belligerent glare disappeared. He shouldered the bag and moved to the door, beginning to feel horror at himself. He said, "Jill, I, I feel I shouldn't have said any of that. . . ."

Kelvin said coldly, "Your feelings do you credit."

Jake stared at him dumbly then left. Kelvin helped Jill to the sofa, saying, "Come over here. You'll be more comfortable. And you'll be safe with me, Jill, safe. I promise it."

She slumped down with her arms on the sofa arm

and her face pressed into them. Suddenly Jake's
voice came through the open door. It sounded
unemotional and ordinary: "Kelvin! Come here a
minute."
"What is it?"
"I forgot to give you something."

Kelvin went to the door, stepped through and
received a blow in the face which sent him stunned
and reeling against the wall. Another blow on the
side of the brow made him sit down on the floor,
hands clasped to head and shaking it to shake off the
dizziness and pain. He heard footsteps receding
downstairs, and got to his feet, staggering and chuckling. He re-entered the room, shutting the door
after him. A lot of blood was flowing onto his
waistcoat. He dabbed his nose with a handkerchief,
laughing and saying, "He punched me! The bugger
punched me!"
He approached Jill who still sobbed into her arms,
and grinned down at her delightedly and threw his
jacket off. He bent and touched her soft hair, shaking his head in wonder and delight and saying, "Oh,
you're so bonny, so bonny!"
The fact that she and he had been bruised by the
same man made him feel they were alike. He walked
away from her, grinning up at the ceiling and saying
with wonder and enthusiasm, "Oh, God, you're
good to me."
He returned to Jill, smearing nose-blood across his
face with the back of a hand, gazing at her and
saying softly, "Oh, Jill, how lovely you are and to
think, and to think, Jill ..."
He walked away, removing tie and waistcoat and

crying at the ceiling, "God, you are good to me, I approve of you, God, I approve of you!"

He returned, laughing happily. She did not heed him. He slid his arms under her and lifted her with a grunt of effort and she lay against his chest, hands covering her face and weeping. He grunted and staggered with her to the bed-table, laughing and saying, "What a weight you are! Oh what a lovely weight she is, God!"

10

THE
SPREAD OF
KELVIN WALKER

During the next days Jill often felt the sensations of a surf-rider among the topmost foam of a huge wave. She and Jake had lived in a static conservative world rocked sometimes by huge explosions which, when the pain of them died down, were seen to have changed nothing, for they were still living the same lives in the same kind of rooms. With Kelvin everything was quick and fluid, always changing into something else and being superseded. The choices he made or got her to make mixed her with so many people and things—shops, taxis, telephones, paperhangers, laundries, banks, credit-accounts, hire-purchase agreements—that she found herself developing new habits, thoughts and appearances. Kelvin and she used much of their time spending or deciding to spend, for he had obtained a great loan from a bank because of the coming marriage. In later years she could never remember Kelvin actually proposing to her yet two days after Jake had left a licence had been got and the date of the wedding fixed, and though Kelvin had done all the talking at the Registry Office she had certainly been there too and answered questions and signed her name.

But changes in Jill were passive responses to the changes around her, she was more fascinated by the changes in Kelvin who was consciously and conscientiously remaking himself. In six days his accent changed from distinct Scots to a form of Anglo-Scots and then grew indistinguishable from BBC English, except during interviews for television when he reverted to his aboriginal Glaik. His bodily movements had been so formally abrupt that they seemed mechanical. Jill decided that this manner had been imposed upon him by living from an early age in cramped conditions with people as assertive as himself, for after acquiring two more rooms on the same floor (another tenant having left about that time) his movements became more casual and absent-minded. He stopped walking to work, arranged to be taken by taxi and spoke of learning to drive. Each day some hint from a magazine or conversation made him discard clusters of old prejudices and take in new ones. Now that he commanded a bedroom, sittingroom and study he needed a lot of new furniture. His taste had originally been for the imitation antique but by the time Jake shattered his earliest purchases his glimpses of modern offices had brought him to feel that good furniture must be clean, simple and efficient. When Jill went with him to the opulent department store where he had opened an account for them he became interested in the work of a firm whose chairs, tables, beds and bookcases were made in smooth light wood with measurements which let them fit crisply together. Jill said, "Please yourself of course. It's your money."

"Don't you like these? Aren't they practical and well made?"

"Yes, but they aren't much fun."

"Is fun an approved element in furnishing nowadays?"

"Approved? If you read more adverts you'd think it was compulsory."

Kelvin asked the salesman for advertising brochures, slipped them into his suitcase, turned to Jill and said, "Today we will not buy furniture. We will buy you clothes—fashionable expensive hats and dresses and shoes."

He stared at her with wide-open mock-dramatic eyes and primly pursed mouth. She began to giggle. He put an arm round her waist and rushed her to the lift.

That year fashion was undergoing the third Victorian Renaissance since the turn of the century. When they came from the ladies' wear department Jill wore a white velvet bodice with a pink knee-length crinoline, calf-length white pantaloons with flounces, a scarlet silk openwork fringed and tasselled shawl, pink satin slippers with ribbons crossed on the ankle, and carried a small pink parasol with a long handle. She said firmly, "Now we'll redecorate you."

"New clothes for me?"

"Of course, I know the telly people want you to always look like an old-fashioned grocer's assistant in his Sunday best but I don't."

Kelvin said thoughtfully, "Yes, there is no reason why my private and public images should correspond. Indeed, a marked contrast between them might be valuable, publicity-wise. Yes, I too shall buy new clothes."

When they left the store arm in arm an hour later

Kelvin wore slim thigh-length boots, tight dove-grey trousers and waistcoat, a black brass-buttoned cut-away tail-coat with high collar, and a sapphire shirt with lavender cravat. He brought his lips to her ear and murmured, "I've often felt grand but till now I never looked it. Isn't it great that we're so conspicuous and grand? Let's go home, let's go home at once."

His love-making lacked Jake's sensitive tact and timing, yet the surprise, delight and energy he brought to it were contagious, most of all on getting home after buying the new clothes. Yet each piece of knowledge and property acquired with such gusto was followed by an almost instantaneous hardening, clarifying and neatening. Jill woke at five next morning and saw him dressed in his old tweed suit, carefully lifting their scattered clothing from the floor and folding it neatly between layers of newspaper. He said sternly, "I should have thought to purchase at least a wardrobe. And in future we will undress carefully."

"For Christ's sake, Kelvin!"

"Yes, yes, it is proper that you side with impulse for you are a woman. But as man and breadwinner my emphasis must be on discipline."

He sat down and began reading the furniture brochures. She pulled the covers over her head and fell asleep.

He woke her next morning with tea, toast and boiled egg on a tray, and walked up and down while she ate.

"I find you are right about fun being an essential ingredient of modern interior design, but there are so many different ways of injecting the ingredient that it is hard to find a single sound rule to guide our choice. One way is to place ugly impractical things among useful nicely made ones. Another is to take well-made simple things and enamel them with bright inharmonious colours. I've decided on a third course."

"Yes?"

He grinned at her. "You must choose the furniture."

"Me?"

"Yes. I will never be able to furnish a fashionably funny room. Nietzsche approves of laughter and so do I, but unluckily humour is not my strong point."

By the end of the week the room had lost all similarity to the former studio. Walls and woodwork were painted white excepting the fireplace wall which was lined with green billiard felt. The floor was covered by a single orange carpet and everything else had either been advertised in the Sunday colour-supplements or bought from expensive junk-shops. And now the hectic flavour began to fade from their lives and when Kelvin was at work Jill busied herself with dusting, tidying, buying food for meals and preparing it. She enjoyed these routines, yet they did not take long, and most of her time was passed reading novels and waiting for Kelvin to come in and decide to do something. She wondered why the days when she did no housework and hung about waiting for Jake had been more interesting. She decided that the interest came from uncertainty about time. When waiting for Jake her reading might continue for ten minutes or an hour or six hours. With Kelvin she had four vacant hours at least five days a week. The books she usually read began to seem trivial and repetitive. She became increasingly fascinated by Kelvin's career. Each time he came home he had something new to tell her about it.

Not the prime minister but the BBC introduced Kelvin to Lord Haversack. One day Hector McKellar said, "I've hooked another big fish for you. The Last Tycoon."
"Haversack?"
"Lord Haversack of Ditch. You'll be frying him next Friday. Take time off till then and do some homework."
"How hard should I be?"
"As hard as you like. He has no friends, only a few dependents and a lot of people who find it wise to keep in touch with him. They'll be the first to laugh when you turn up the heat. Of course I don't expect you to conduct a muckraking probe. That might stir up dirt which would stick to everyone and bring The Prevailing Consensus down on our heads like a ton of bricks. Go for the personality clash, but stay on the safe side of the libel law. Drop a hint or two. He keeps a permanent house-guest at his home on the Riviera."

Haversack looked ancient yet boyish. His bald head and face resembled a bag which had been savagely crumpled then pumped up with not quite enough air to remove the creases. His accent was mid-Atlantic. His stature was two inches less than Dylan Jones's but Kelvin found him more impressive. On the morning of the interview it became public knowledge that the most ambitiously daring

of all his financial bids had been defeated by an ally
deserting to his competitors, yet that evening he
faced Kelvin and the cameras with an air of casual
amusement which would have been equally appropriate had he been victorious. Kelvin said, "This
has been a hard day for you, Lord Haversack."

"Not at all. I've lost nothing. I've just failed to gain
the little extra I was aiming for. There are no alltime
winners in the business world."

"May I remind the viewer," said Kelvin, smiling
unevenly at the camera, "that the little extra referred
to is the ownership of *The Guardian* and *The Times*.
What did you intend to do with these papers, Lord
Haversack?"

"Merge them."

"Why? Each of them is running at a profit. Each has
a devoted readership."

"I know, but by merging them I would have re-
leased money that could have been more profitably
invested elsewhere."

"Invested in what?"

"Betting shops. Betting shops, bingo parlours, and
casinos."

"But, Lord Haversack . . ." cried Kelvin.

"Knew that would shock you," said Haversack,
chuckling slightly. "You'll be telling me next that
these newspapers are more than entertainment, they
are important sources of public information."

"Yes, that is exactly what I was going to tell you. Is
it not true?"

"Not at all. Nowadays people get their information
from television—from programmes like this, Mr
Walker. You should never under-rate yourself, Mr
Walker. In future people like you will provide the
public with its information, and people like me will

provide them with everything else. That is what most people want so why quarrel with them? You and I are both democrats, I hope."

Kelvin noticed he was losing this contest. His questions were becoming reactions to Haversack's answers instead of the other way round. He questioned less and listened more. Once or twice he chuckled approvingly. Haversack expanded and said, "You see, owning a lot of newspapers is not a way of wielding power, it's a way of making money. Like most people I don't give a damn about politics. I leave politics to my editors. I've editors of every shade of political opinion, and each one is allowed to say what he likes, if it isn't treason or blasphemy."
"You are a Christian?"
"I try to be. This is a Christian nation, I hope."
"But you don't practise Christian charity," said Kelvin, pleasantly.
"What do you mean?"
"Your most popular papers spread scurrilous gossip about people in the entertainment industry. Your reporters skulk behind garden hedges and photograph bedroom windows, yet they take a very high and censorious moral tone."
"And so they should!" said Haversack. "Who will denounce adultery and perversion if the popular press remain silent? If I impose a policy on my papers it is only this—to defend the decent standards of ordinary people everywhere."
Kelvin said, "Why consider thou the mote in thy brother's eye, and consider not the beam which is in thine own?"
Haversack's mouth fell open. Kelvin said helpfully, "Saint Matthew wrote that."

After a moment Haversack said in a low voice, "What has Saint Matthew to do with me?"

"Nothing, Lord Haversack. I have read nothing in your papers which hints at irregularities in your own private life so it must be absolutely above suspicion. Do you not agree with me?"

Haversack sat back in his chair, watchful yet brooding. Kelvin said goodnight to the audience and the programme ended.

But the participants stayed seated. Haversack eventually nodded twice and said, "You did that well."

"Thank you," said Kelvin, "you were a tough opponent. I scored a good last-minute goal but you won the match."

"I did, did I?" said Haversack thoughtfully, and a moment later added, "Why have I never met you before?"

"I don't know. Dylan Jones offered to introduce us. I was perfectly prepared for that. Perhaps he forgot."

"He offered to introduce us, did he? What else did he offer?"

"Our conversation was private but of course he spoke to me like a politician."

After a pause Haversack said, "I'm giving a little luncheon party at the Dorchester next Sunday, you should come to it. You'll meet a few smart men who will be interested to meet you."

"No," said Kelvin, "My public image will be a decidedly puritan one after tonight. I only threw the Bible at you because I had no other ammunition, but from now on people will expect me to be a bit biblical. Until I am thoroughly at home in the part I had better avoid smart company at the Dorchester,

whatever that is. But there can be no harm in a purely private meeting."
They arranged one.

While preparing for bed that night Kelvin gave Jill his news in a voice very different from the firm, discreet voice he had used when talking to Haversack. He said, "So he and I are lunching tomorrow in a club which is so exclusive that it has no name, no address and almost nobody knows it exists!"
Jill said, "Why?"
"Why what?"
"Why does he want to talk to you? Why do you want to talk to him?"
"Surely that is obvious."
"Not to me."
Kelvin sighed patiently. He said, "I am a very clever fellow. Clever fellows need clever fellows. Lord Haversack, like Hector McKellar and Dylan Jones, realizes I can be useful to him."
"But," said Jill, and fell silent.
"But what? But what?"
"The first time we ate together you seemed to look down on people who were tools—tools of business-men and politicians, that is."
"I still look down on such people," said Kelvin stiffly, "and if at present I do not despise myself as completely as you do—please don't interrupt me!—it is because I am serving an apprenticeship. I am learning my way toward."
"Toward what?"
He climbed into bed, lay with his back to her and refused to say another word, but Jill was incapable of quarrelling with a sulky child. She slid beneath the sheets, snuggled up to his back, laid an arm over

him and fell asleep. Next morning they ate breakfast in friendship again.

But when Kelvin, with springing stride, returned from his business lunch next afternoon he did not go at once upstairs to Jill, he descended to the back basement and tapped on Mrs Hendon's door. She opened and said, "Oo, Mr Walker, I wish you'd given me warning. Just look at how I look! I'm always this way when not expecting somebody."

"I call on a matter of business," said Kelvin entering, "urgent business. A pink nylon wrap-round dressing gown will not disconcert me. Thrust it from your mind. You typewrite. Can you take dictation?"

"Well yes, it so happens I have had that training."

"Good. A pattern emerges. Please listen carefully. I am about to become (among other things) a part-time journalist. I have no fluency with the pen but they tell me I have an almost inspirational gift of the gab. I want to employ you at the going rate for a few hours a week. On Saturday morning you will come to my study. I will pace up and down spouting whatever enters my head upon such topics as the miniskirt, the singing beetles, bearded flower-power student revolutionaries spoonfed from the taxpayers' pocket by the permissive attitude of a welfare bureaucracy run mad, and of course, the greed of the unions. I will not refer to the greed of the stock exchange and the legal and managerial professions. You and I understand, Mrs Hendon, that countries are made prosperous by the acquisitiveness of propertied people and made poor by the acquisitiveness of everyone else, but not all possess the intelligence to see this. And do not think my spoutings will be glumly political. They will amuse, they will stimulate rather than pedantically inform. I will mock the follies of the age from the standpoint of the decent, down-to-earth, respectable, ordinary man in the street, backing my remarks with an occasional biblical quotation. You will write down my words until I run out of words, Mrs Hendon, then you will go away, type them and bring them back to me. I will then underline the golden nuggets among what will initially be a sad mass of dross, Mrs Hendon, I will link these nuggets with some clean new lines of verbiage, you will type a fair copy of the revision (and if the Lord wills it) our article will be printed throughout the length and breadth of Great Britain. Are you amenable, Mrs Hendon? Think well before you reply. I warn you here and now, that if you serve under me I will drive you hard."

Mrs Hendon said, "Yes, well, I am amenable, if it's at the going rate. And I don't mind being pushed about a bit if it's done polite like, and in a good cause. You want me to start Saturday?"

"To be frank Mrs Hendon, I would like to start now, if you are free. I am inspired. I am swelling and bubbling with notions. Take them down for me please!"

"Wait half a tick while I get my pad and pencil," said Mrs Hendon efficiently.

Kelvin walked round and round the table in the middle of the room. The low ceiling and tidy, cramped surroundings suddenly reminded him of his home in Glaik, but with an odd difference. This was a room where he was master. Mrs Hendon, pad and pencil on lap, watched him ardently from an armchair in the corner. He wondered if his father

had ever felt like this before breaking into prayer:
dominant yet humble: commissioned by the power
which ruled the universe, and with an audience
waiting for his words, yet temporarily speechless
because the words had not arrived. "The only problem is the first sentence," Lord Haversack had said.
"When you've discovered that everything else
follows naturally."

"From the earliest," said Kelvin
suddenly, "days of recorded history it has been a widely accepted
fact that . . ."

He dried up and tried again.

"The English comma, the Scots
comma, the Welsh and yes
comma, even the Irish live on an
island comma, and from the
earliest days of recorded
history it has been recognized
that an island is a piece of land
completely surrounded by . . ."

He dried up, groaned and struck his brow with his
fist. Mrs Hendon murmured, "Perhaps a cuppa
would help. Shall I pop a bag in a mug for you?"
"Shush!" said Kelvin,

"Today we live in a very queer
world comma, a world which
would have astonished not just
our ancestors but ourselves if we
had seen it ten or twelve years ago
period. Who then would have
believed in the possibility of the

teabag comma, instant coffee
powder comma, cardboard milk
bottles and the Sputnik query."

Suddenly the words were flowing. From a survey of
the commonplace and concrete he soared up and
seized issues which were threatening to tear the
world apart. His article became a manifesto, an open
declaration of faith.

"In the present century dash—
except in time of war dash—our
leaders have been content to drift
with the current rather than
set their faces against it period.
How unlike the politicians of
Victorian times comma, the
Palmsburies and Shaftstones
(check these names Mrs
Hendon) who made Britain
Great because they Believed
capital 'g' at Great capital 'b'
at Believed exclamation mark
and start new paragraph.
"There is clearly no hope at
all for the country in Marxism
and Maoism and Women's
Liberation and Gay Liberation
and all the other isms and tions
which bedevil the age period.
Belief there must be comma,
but let us abandon mere
limited earthly beliefs and
believe comma, once and for
all comma, in . . ."

The light went out of his countenance. He bit his lip and strolled pondering round the table. Mrs Hendon, softly prompting, murmured "... and believe, once and for all, in .. ?"
Kelvin stood still, frowned at his shoes, beamed at the ceiling and cried,

> "... and believe comma, once
> and for all comma, in Belief
> itself capital 'b' for Belief ex-
> clamation mark! And end of
> article."

"Beautiful words, Mr Walker!" said Mrs Hendon, "really beautiful."
"No! Mrs Hendon," said Kelvin severely, "not beautiful, but true, which is better. I leave you to type that out. Without claiming that what I have just dictated is all pure gold I think we will discover less dross between the nuggets than anticipated. Haversack will like it. I withdraw. I am exhausted."

He went upstairs to Jill with an unusually solemn tread. He was awestruck by the new talent he had discovered in himself.

11
THE FALL

Over breakfast one morning Kelvin took a card from an envelope, read it carefully then said, "It will be necessary for you to purchase a new dress, hat, shoes, coat, stockings, etcetera. We must spend a lot of money on them because you must look conventional yet extraordinary."

"Why?" said Jill.

He handed her the card. It said that Her Majesty the Queen had commanded the Lord Chancellor to invite Kelvin Walker and Lady to a garden party at Buckingham Palace, Morning Wear, Uniform or Lounge Suit. Jill was delighted. She said, "How does the Queen know about you and me?"

"She probably doesn't. Dylan Jones will have arranged it."

"And will she talk to us?"

"We will stand in a kind of queue and when we get to her she will shake our hand and say she is pleased to see us. There is a matter which weighs on me slightly. It is hardly worth mentioning but it concerns the tea. I have told you I prefer two spoonfuls of sugar in my cup and for the last three days you have given me one. I have not referred to this till now in the hope that it was a temporary aberration,

and as I said, the matter is not worth mentioning. . . ."
"So why mention it?"
"Because though not worth mentioning it is worth
bearing in mind."
Jill pondered this for a little then pushed the
sugar-bowl toward him and returned the card saying
wistfully, "Are you not excited, Kelvin?"
"About the invitation? No, but I'm satisfied. It is
another step in the right direction. I have taken
several of them lately."

She knew what he meant. He had made himself
a figure of nationwide renown by taking a strong
stand on all the emotionally charged issues which
did not divide the main political parties. That evening he would be appearing on a current affairs programme, not to interview but be interviewed. None
of this greatly interested Jill because it had come to
seem inevitable and did not involve her. Kelvin had
said their domestic life must remain private at
present because from a clerical standpoint they were
living in sin, but things would change after the
marriage.

Suddenly she remembered something which made
her feel cheerful. She said, "Jake 'phoned last
night—I forgot to tell you."
"Jake?" said Kelvin, puzzled. It took him a moment
to remember who Jake was but Jill did not notice
this. She said, "He was perfectly friendly and cheerful—I told him about our wedding, and he laughed
and said he supposed the best man had won and to
give you his congratulations. And guess what! He's
working as a bus conductor."
"Indeed."

"But today is his day off so I asked him round for a meal this evening—before you go off to that show, you know."

"I have no wish to see him," said Kelvin grimly. "He humiliated us both. I cannot forget that. And I am astonished at your absence of pride in asking him to eat here."

Jill was also astonished. She looked hard at Kelvin to see if he was absolutely serious, then spoke seriously herself.

"Jake is my best friend, Kelvin, even if he is no longer my lover. You aren't going to change that. I always liked him and I always will. And he liked you! He gave you this room to live in when you had even less than we had! Have you forgotten?"

"I admit I have reasons to be grateful to him," said Kelvin coldly, "but I never liked him and never will. It would be dishonest to pretend otherwise. See him tonight if you must, but I will not be here. I'll simply send a car to collect you for the show."

Once again she felt he had wrapped up matters in a neat verbal parcel which left her nothing to say. She muttered, "I don't think I want to see this show."

"You must. It will be a turning point."

He left the table, picked up a necktie and carefully knotted it on before a mirror over the mantelpiece. He sighed and said, "This wedding is a pity, in a way."

Jill stared at him.

"Do you want to put it off?"

"Of course not, we've no time for postponement, we must be married when we meet the Queen. But a church would be far more suitable than a registry office."

"Why? You don't believe in God and I don't believe in religion. Why?"

"I never said I did not believe in God, I said I was against him. I also said he was dead. But he came alive again on the night when I finally obtained you."

Jill covered her eyes with a hand. His mildly tuneful, careful voice went on saying things which he clearly thought were reasonable but which made her feel she was in a bad dream.

"Do you remember that night? I found myself, in the heat of the moment, talking to God in a mood of considerable appreciation, and doing so quite voluntarily, or rather, involuntarily, because I did not notice I was doing it. It was not like praying at home in Glaik because the thing I was talking to—the not quite human thing in the room with us—no longer hated me. It approved. Since then I have had to ask myself, did I manage to get all I ever wanted—work, love, fame, money, power and a home of my own—did I manage to get all these in a few weeks through the strength of my own unaided will? The answer is clearly, no. I am not naturally as sublime and irresistible as I became when I at last got you. Am I?"

"No," said Jill.

"No," said Kelvin, buttoning his jacket before the mirror and surveying the result with satisfaction. "No, there was a higher power at work. From the very start, even when least aware of it, I had been a mere glove on the hand of He who engendered the hoary frost of heaven and out of Whose womb came ice. It was a humbling discovery."

"For Pete's sake come off it, Kelvin!" cried Jill vehemently.

"There are times," he murmured, "when you say

things that make me feel a million miles away from
you."

He lifted his briefcase and umbrella and went to
the door. He said, "You should read my articles in
the papers. You should watch me on the box. You
should study my fan mail. There are those who like
me for my divine certainties, people who like living
in a lawful universe with a real ceiling over their
head. This evening I will defend my newfound faith
before a really big audience for the first time. I need
you in that audience, Jill, I need to feel you near
me. You are my luck. You brought me to God. He
made you for precisely that purpose. You *must* come
to me, tonight."
"I'll only come," cried Jill wildly, "if Jake comes
too."
He looked at her for a moment, then said, "All right,
bring him if you wish. But you are a strange, strange
woman."
Then he went off to work.

On his desk at the BBC lay an envelope marked
Revision of current schedule. He read the contents
then 'phoned Hector McKellar. He said, "Hector,
this new schedule. What do you mean by it?"
"Surely that is obvious? But if you insist on dis-
cussing the matter I will see you at three-thirty."
"Not sooner?"
"No."
"Right. Three-thirty."
Kelvin sat brooding for a while. The new schedule
indicated that for the next three weeks he would be
interviewing no figures of political or social importance. He made some 'phone calls then went to the

staff club. As he entered it most of the conversations briefly halted then resumed more quietly in his vicinity and more loudly farther away. He was now accustomed to alterations in the companies he joined. He sensed a new note of enquiry and speculation in the attention obliquely directed at him. He drank a sweet black coffee, smiling slightly and feeling the excitement of a confident man before a worthwhile battle. Then he returned to his office and made more 'phone calls.

At three-thirty Hector McKellar told him bluntly, "You are going too fast for us, Kelvin."

"Who do you mean by 'us,' Hector?"

"In the narrow sense of the word I mean The Prevailing Consensus. In the wider sense I mean the British Public."

"But I am not travelling too fast for the public! A great part of it is behind me. Have you seen my viewing figures, Hector?"

"But you have forgotten why we employed you, Kelvin. At the outset I gave you a very special role. You were to undermine the bigwigs, but you were to do it almost by accident, from no particular standpoint—"

"That sort of undermining changes *nothing*, Hector."

"Exactly! Which is why we encourage it. But in your interview last night with the shadow minister of birth control it was deliberate cruelty to dredge up the business of her first marriage."

"I think not, Hector. It would be a disgrace if family planning in Britain were to be brought under the rule of one who has scorned the sacrament of matrimony."

"And what about your campaign to drive the body out of advertising?"

"To drive THE DIVINE IMAGE out of advertising."

"I'm as Scottish as you are, Kelvin!" said McKellar with a touch of anger. "I am well aware that mankind—and to a lesser extent, womankind—is made in the image of God."

"Then does it not offend you, Hector, that this body—" Kelvin slapped his chest—"this container of all we can ever truly know and love—is being used as bait by shopkeepers? The women of Britain are behind me on this one, both the extreme feminists and the Housewives for Decency movement."

"And British Industry is against you."

"Industry is not sacred, Hector. It exists to give us coats and potato crisps and refrigerators and motor cars. If it cannot do so without trespassing on our most heartfelt instincts then it compels me to oppose it. Which I do."

After a moment McKellar spoke as if introducing a completely new topic. He said casually, "I've been empowered to offer you a salary increase of six thousand a year if you will stop writing for the press and return to Vox Pop for six months or so. With a few of the more straightforward kinds of interview from time to time of course."

"And of course," said Kelvin, "you will make sure I interview nobody of importance whose views differ greatly from my own. I'm sorry, Hector. I am not in this game for the money."

McKellar chuckled and said, "Good lad! I told them you were not to be bought."

He lit a cigarette and leaned back in his chair as if

there was no more to be said. Kelvin had a sensation of something missing. He said, "If my services are an embarrassment to the BBC I can always seek other channels, Hector."

"Of course!" said McKellar, "So you can. We'll discuss that tomorrow, perhaps. Tonight we're giving you a whole hour of peak viewing time to speak for yourself. After tonight there will be no holding you—will there? By the way we've changed tonight's chairman."

"Who will it be?"

"Me."

"You?"

"Yes. It's a few years since I've actually appeared on the box myself but this is a special occasion. Remember, we're both lads from Glaik. I know how your mind works better than anyone else in these latitudes."

Kelvin left the office in an unusually thoughtful mood.

Meanwhile a restrained reunion was taking place in W.C.12. Jill opened the door to an impressive but friendly figure in the uniform of the London transport authority. He carried a large bouquet of perfect crimson roses and her delight at the sight of him was so great that for a moment she was unable to speak. He said lightly, "A wedding bouquet."

She said, "Kelvin's had to go to the BBC. Let's have a drink."

She poured him a large malt whisky and brought it to the leather armchair where he had seated himself, then picked up the flowers and smelt them.

"These are lovely. Thank you."

"I'm working. I can afford them."

"Do you hate it?"

"The work? No, I like it. I like any job for the first week or two. It's when I get used to it that I can't stand it."

He stared into the glass and said, "Jill, I ... I hope you'll be very happy with him."

Her face lit up. She said breathlessly, "Do you, Jake?"

He nodded.

"Then you love me?"

"There's no point in talking about that."

She turned her back to him to hide her delight and tried to speak casually. She said, "I'm not going to marry him, Jake."

Jake was startled.

"Why not?"

"I'm afraid of him."

"Why?"

"Hasn't it struck you that I'm the first girl he spoke to in London and this is the first house he visited? I've begun to think that no matter what girl he spoke to first he'd have married her, no matter what house he visited he'd have taken it over."

"Come off it, Jill, that's impossible. It's insane."

"That's what's so frightening. There's something wrong with his way of looking at the world. It wasn't too bad when he talked about Nietzsche but now he's onto God and it's worse, much worse. I don't think he's properly human."

"Who is? I'm not."

"Kelvin thinks he's perfect and it makes him ... horribly strong. Have you a place where you could put me up?"

"Yes, but surely you won't walk out on him here and now!"

"Yes," said Jill. "I didn't know I was going to do it before I opened the door to you. I couldn't see how much I've come to detest him before I opened the door to you. But now it's obvious."

For half an hour Jake, moved by that self-denying impulse which surfaces in most people when they are absolutely certain of getting what they want, argued on Kelvin's behalf. He was eventually won over to Jill's view in all but this: he thought she should not simply walk out of the house but should see Kelvin and bid him goodbye. At last she said, "All right. He wants me in the studio audience for some rotten show he's doing tonight. If you come with me I'll tell him after it. Meanwhile I'll pack my things. A BBC car is picking us up. We'll get the chauffeur to make a detour so that we can drop them at your place."

She flung open a wardrobe and several drawers and began spreading dresses, suits, slacks and all sorts of underwear over the furniture.

"He's bought you a lot," said Jake, slightly chilled by her efficiency.

"Yes, he was good that way," said Jill.

"Don't you think you should leave some of it?"

"Certainly not, I've earned all this by being a housewife and bedwarmer. By the way, are you short of anything? Do you need sheets or towels?"

The announcer always introduced *Feedback* as, "A television programme about the makers of television—a programme in which a cross-section of the public question the celebrities from behind the scenes and in front of the cameras."

The public cross-section varied from week to week but always harmonized with the public manner of the celebrity. Comedians were questioned in an atmosphere of facetious badinage, singers in one of lyrical sentimentality, producers in one of portentous blandness. There was no doubt at all that a cutting questioner like Kelvin Walker would be cuttingly questioned, but almost nobody who knew him doubted his ability to talk any questioner into the ground. The programme had only one convention which sometimes caused surprise. Not all questioners were announced beforehand and the subject of the programme did not meet them before live transmission, so viewers had once enjoyed the astonishment of Hillbilly Henderson when confronted by the Archbishop of Canterbury, who turned out to be his greatest fan. Such theatrical touches were heightened by a dim little Roman circus of a studio with strong low lighting on three chairs in the centre. Kelvin sat down on one to the sound of big applause, some real, some canned. He tried to see where Jill was sitting and failed. The nearest row of people looked like a line of black silhouettes and the furthest away merged with the red and green shadows they cast on a wall of surrounding screens.

Hector McKellar sat opposite him and when silence fell said, "Good evening. A notable feature of the last few weeks has been the rise to public eminence of Kelvin Walker, partly through his articles in the popular press but mainly through his idiosyncrasies as a television interviewer. In the studio tonight we have parents, teachers, psychiatrists and clergymen who are all keen critics of Kelvin's preachings, and in the course of our informal discussion I intend to call each one forward to give them a fair crack of the critical whip. But I want to

begin myself by asking Kelvin to admit that the
sentiments he expresses are all reactionary ones."
Kelvin smiled and said, "No. Oh no."
"You don't admit it?"
"No, I insist on it. When you say 'reactionary' you
mean 'old-fashioned' and I'm glad I'm that. It puzzles me that Victorian architecture and ornament
have grown popular again but people are still
ashamed of the Victorian morality."
"So they should be. Victorian morality was a harsh
and punitive morality."
"A morality which is unwilling to hang murderers
and flog thieves does not deserve the name."
"Do you really believe criminals can be reformed by
corporal punishment?"
"Of course not. We do not punish the wicked in
order to reform them—that's almost impossible—
we do it to make the righteous feel more confident.
Savage punishment is a way of asserting the difference between virtue and vice. By abandoning it we
have come to feel that the good and bad are essen-
tially alike, so both sorts have become less sure of
themselves. The wicked accuse the good of treating
them badly, the good beat their breasts and beg for-
giveness. Bringing back the birch will restore the
self-esteem of *everybody*."
"Are you suggesting that even criminals approve of
savage punishments?" said McKellar.
"Indeed I am," said Kelvin. "A thief must feel very
superior and cunning when he steals something. If
you catch him and treat him as a sick man you rob
him of his self respect."
"Do you apply that rule to the education of children?"
"Of course! If children are never punished they

never feel loved. My own father—" He hesitated, and for the first time that evening a shadow of doubt touched his face.

"Your own father?" said McKellar softly.

"My own father was, is, I mean, I mean my own father is a very stern man. As a boy I feared him. I have lived to be glad of it."

Hector McKellar raised a forefinger. He said, "I had meant to introduce your father into this discussion rather later in the programme but this seems an appropriate moment. Will you come forward Mr Walker?"

One of the blackest silhouettes in the front row of the audience stood up and walked into the circle of light. He was an erect little man in black homburg, black overcoat, trousers, waistcoat, boots and celluloid collar with tartan tie. He grasped a large umbrella like a surveyor carrying a piece of important equipment. Ignoring his son absolutely he sat in the remaining chair and stared hard at Hector McKellar, hands crossed on the handle of the umbrella planted vertically between his legs, chin resting on hands. His peculiar appearance was exceeded, however, by his effect upon Kelvin's aghast face and body which, rocking from side to side in his chair, exhibited the contortions of a small child ardently desiring attention while being terrified of attracting it. In a faint voice he said, "Father."

"Good evening, Mr Walker," said Hector McKellar.

"Father!" said Kelvin.

"Mr Walker," said McKellar, "you have heard how highly your son esteems you. What do you think of *him*?"

"He is a hypocrite," said Mr Walker in the hard, dull, toneless voice of one fixed in a state of sullen, steady and unrelenting anger. Kelvin raised his right hand to shoulder level, urgently wagged the fingers and said timidly, "I'm glad to see you, father!"

Only the cameras paid him any attention. McKellar said, "Why a hypocrite?"

Mr Walker smiled bitterly.

"Because I have seen him bend the knee at family prayers, and bow his head and pretend to murmur words with his mouth, when all the time there was nothing in his heart but emptiness and black rebellion. I did not remark upon it at the time for remark would have done no good, but if ever a man was outcast from the Godly and their ways that man was Kelvin Walker."

"Father, I've changed," said Kelvin.

"What did you do about this, Mr Walker?" asked McKellar.

"Naturally I did all I could. I deprived him of the education which would have given his viciousness scope, and kept him as close beside me as possible. By giving him only a shilling a week pocket money I stopped him frequenting the picture houses and billiard salons, the drinking dens and domino parlours to which his pagan spirit would naturally have led him. Nonetheless he contrived to bypass these precautions by visiting a public library and battening on only God knows what pernicious rubbish. Then one day—in circumstances I am ashamed to mention—he ran from home without a word of warning. And that was the last I heard of him before a customer *congratulated* me on my son's appearance on television. But I always knew there was no good in the lad."

"Father," said Kelvin.

"Mr Walker, what is your objection to Kelvin appearing on television?" asked McKellar.

"Am I right in thinking it may make him a figure of national importance?"

"The signs point that way."

"Power, Mr McKellar, can only be used well by men with faith. Understand me, I am not a bigot, their faith need not be my faith. They can have faith in passing a law or abolishing a law, in fighting an opponent or making an ally, in getting money or spending money, but if they have faith in something outside themselves they will only do the world the normal amount of harm."

The old man raised his voice jeeringly and looked straight at Kelvin for the first time.

"My son has faith in nothing but his own desires!" he cried. "He is a hollow shell stuffed with nothing but self-conceit and blown onward by the wind of the pride of Lucifer!"

"But, father, I've changed!" cried Kelvin. "I'm not wicked any more!"

He had forgotten all about the cameras, the studio audience and everyone else. He leaned eagerly toward the only power in the world he had ever really dreaded, certain that a few rightly chosen words would make it his ally.

And the power, on an unexpectedly intimate gloating note, said, "What about the forty pounds you stole from me?"

"I can repay them, father, I can repay them here and now!" cried Kelvin, thrusting hard into the breast of his jacket.

"And the jewellery? The few poor trinkets that your

mother treasured and I treasured in remembrance of her?"

"I have the pawn tickets here!" said Kelvin pulling out his wallet. "I can redeem them anytime! Anytime! I've just been so busy I forgot!"

"Do you know, Mr McKellar, I have never been inside a pawnshop in my life?" said Mr Walker, almost conversationally. "My youth was a poor one. My parents were poor people. But they taught me to shun a pawnshop as I would shun a brothel. Yet my son who has never wanted for food and clothing and shelter and a clean bed, is not ashamed to pass his dead mother's few poor trinkets over a pawnshop counter in return for ... how much money did they give you?"

"I needed that money," sobbed Kelvin wildly, "and my mother wouldn't have minded. I think maybe she loved me."

"I love you, Kelvin!" roared Mr Walker at a pitch which made three sound technicians wrench off their earphones. "Why else am I destroying you like this?"

A moment later, since nobody had answered his question, he said on a reasonably calm note, "To prevent you destroying *yourself*! A grocer's assistant is all you are fit for. When you have learned to walk humbly before God you may try for something else, but not before."

With a sudden moan of indrawn breath Kelvin shut his eyes and mouth very tight, clasped his hands behind his skull with arms compressing his ears, lifted his knees to his chin and compressed himself as nearly into an egg-shape as an angular man could. For a moment Hector McKellar feared this egg might roll off the chair but putting out a probing hand he found it muscularly rigid and perfectly stable. An uneasy murmur rose from the audience. Apparently the spectacle had thrilled but also disgusted them. The time had come to end it. McKellar stood up and said, "This comes as a very great shock. Clearly Kelvin Walker, like many greater men, approves of a code he lacks the strength to embody, but I know I speak for everyone when I say that in losing our respect he has certainly gained our sympathy."

"You bastard!" screamed a woman in the audience. It was Jill. McKellar nodded and shrugged slightly. He believed that the stability of all well-conducted societies depended on bastards like himself. He said, "I'm sorry that the programme is finishing fifty minutes ahead of schedule. I'm sure that Presentation, with its usual thoroughness, will be able to fill the remaining period of time with a little light music. However, there will be a discussion of to-night's *Feedback* on *Late Night Line Up* at 11.20 after the news. Good evening, ladies and gentlemen."

12
EXODUS

Kelvin had tied his body in a knot for two reasons. One was to shield it from the flaying glance of the studio audience and of those extra millions who were surveying him through the cameras, the other was to protect a precious core of certainty from the shattering contempt of his father. He heard the studio audience leaving. He heard Hector McKellar wonder aloud if medical help was necessary. He heard his father say that his condition was not new—he had always gone like that after a good thrashing, and always took ten or twelve minutes to recover. He heard Jill say, "We're friends—can we help?" and McKellar say on a surprised note, at a distance, "He has friends?"

A light hand touched his head and Jill said, "Oh Kelvin. Oh Kelvin."

His father said, "Pity won't help him."

A bit later Kelvin said, "How many are there now Dad?"

His father said, "Only two. You can come out son." He spoke in the firmly tender voice he had always used after giving a beating. Kelvin untied himself.

He placed his feet on the floor and hunched for-

ward over his fist, biting his thumb-knuckle and
furiously thinking. His father was still in the adja-
cent chair. Jake and Jill stood nearby, otherwise the
great space was empty and lit by an even and ordinary light. Mr Walker got to his feet and said, "Well
now, are you ready to come home?"
Kelvin stood up automatically. Jill shouted, "You
surely aren't going home with *him*, Kelvin?"
Jake said, "Listen, Kelvin, nothing very unusual
happened here tonight. The bastards gave you a
job because you were useful to them, then when
they found you were working for yourself they
screwed you up—that happens in Britain all the
time. So don't worry, mate! You'll get another
job."
Jill said, "Yes, stay here. Stay here with us. What
do silly speeches on television matter? All that matters is freedom. What life will you have with *that*
poisonous old man?"
Mr Walker grinned sarcastically. Kelvin stared from
Jill to Jake and back again. They were obviously
halves of a single couple again. He told Jill flatly,
"*You* don't love me."
She whispered, "I'm sorry."
He said, "Please leave. You have become irrelevant.
Go away! Go away with *him*. I have worse things
than human treachery to contend with."
She stared at him and wept, injured in the tenderest
part of herself which was her desire to help. Jake
placed his arm around her shoulder, sighed and shook
his head at Kelvin, then led her away.

However, Kelvin did not meekly follow his father
toward a different exit. He began walking backward
and forward, snapping his fingers and passionately

muttering. "Why did He do it? I would be perfectly happy if I understood His reason for it."

"He meant to drive you out of public life," said Mr Walker, slightly disconcerted. His son no longer had the manner of a frightened child. Kelvin glanced at him coldly and said, "Who are you referring to?"

"To your boss."

"Which one?"

"Hector McKellar, of course."

"*I* was referring to God."

Mr Walker was greatly startled. He said, "Kelvin! Do you tell me that at last you ... believe?"

"Have you not read my words in the papers?"

"Indeed! And they would have been greatly to my taste had I not thought them the words of a graceless hypocrite."

"You were wrong, father. Divine Grace was manifest in the first big success of my career. Since then my faith has never wavered. How else could I have done so well? Without faith I would have been as sounding brass and tinkling cymbal."

"Without charity."

Kelvin said, "I don't understand you."

"The apostle said a lack of charity made us brazen."

Kelvin shook his head.

"I'm sure that statement is a mistranslation. Faith can move mountains but charity has very little practical value."

"Kelvin!" said Mr Walker, awestruck, "I have sometimes thought that!"

His son looked at him for a moment then said, "You had better come home with me."

Jill had removed her personal belongings and

some handy items which Kelvin would never use, otherwise she had left the apartment exactly as he liked to find it. Mr Walker was greatly impressed. He walked about stroking the fabrics of the furniture, examining the base of ornaments and peeping into drawers. His son sat upon the sofa, sighing and pondering the inscrutable ways of the Almighty. Mr Walker located the fridge and cooker and made them a meal. As he poured out the tea he asked, "Did you get all this on hire purchase?"

"No, I paid for it by bankloan."

"Good. That is the cheapest way. When I chose to assist in your public demolition I thought you were on your way to everlasting fire. I was too hasty."

"You talk like a child, father," cried Kelvin. "You did not choose to demolish me, you were chosen! Surely you! a session clerk! must realize that everything which happens is part of God's plan. Everyone in the world labours upon that plan. But now and again there arises one who can feel the plan in his very bones. For several weeks I was the biggest bulldozer on the Divine building site, nobody could withstand me. Surely it is no part of the Eternal Purpose to drive this splendid piece of machinery—" Kelvin smote his chest—"into the mud!"

"Kelvin," said his father, "perhaps God has work for you in Scotland."

"Scotland?"

"A poor province," said Mr Walker. "A neglected province. A despised province. But four hundred years back we conceived ourselves to be a Chosen People. We had a leader then."

Kelvin said thoughtfully, "A Chosen People," and pinched his underlip between thumb and forefinger. He said, "Remind me of my assets, father."

"Assets," said Mr Walker. "Well, you have not
quarrelled with the press, and such is the corruption
of the age that your performance tonight may make
even more people keen to read you. The BBC wishes
to drop you but since you have broken no contract
they will be obliged to make you a fairly big financial settlement. Meanwhile your notoriety will shut
no gates into other television companies, if you
adopt a suitable posture."

"Which is?"

"Repentance."

"Of course. I will repent openly and thoroughly.
Many good careers have been based on an early repentance. John Knox was once a Catholic priest,
and Saint Paul a pagan Greek, and Moses an Egyp-
tian prince. All began by oppressing or scorning
their own people but they repented. Publicly. Tell
me, father, if I return to Scotland how will I be
received?"

Mr Walker said, "I believe you will be welcomed.
You have become famous but have also made a fool
of yourself. The one will enable your countrymen to
forgive you the other."

"And vice versa?"

"And vice versa."

"Father," said Kelvin, "I feel it again. In my very
bones."

"The plan?"

"The plan. I must return to Glaik and put my hand
to the plough."

"Glaik?"

"Why not? It is equidistant from Aberdeen where
the oil is, and Edinburgh where the capital is, and
Glasgow where the television is. I may even decide
to enter the ministry. Or perhaps not. It might

impede me when I tackle the Catholic question. And it may be necessary, later on, to make elbow room for ourselves by detaching Scotland from the British Isles."

"Geographically?" said his father, looking worried. Kelvin laughed heartily.

"No! Politically. Don't worry, Dad. I haven't lost my grip on reality."

"Then there is only one matter outstanding between us," said Mr Walker, and raised a warning fore-finger. "I refer to the young lady you dismissed from that BBC place with a flea in her lug. You mentioned love to her. I know nothing about it but suspect the worst. You will get no support from me if you involve yourself in another lawless liaison."

"I have sufficiently plumbed the fickle depths of the female heart," said Kelvin, grimly, "I will have no further carnal knowledge of women before I have bound one legally to me."

So they returned to Scotland.

13
ANTICLIMAX

With his father's support he took evening classes,
did some freelance journalism, followed his brothers
to university and became first a student, and then a
doctor of divinity. He was ordained minister to a
church in Glaik, then Glasgow, then Edinburgh.
Hard-hitting sermons on radio and television
brought him widespread attention. He is now the
official spokesman for all that is most restrictive in
Scottish religious and social opinion. The public,
the press, and even his opponents love and respect
him for the predictability of his utterances on any
topic whatsoever. While friendly with the leaders
of most Scottish political parties he is a member of
none, though he sits upon extremely important
public committees as a counterbalance to a succes-
sion of not very radical socialists. He counter-
balances so successfully that the important public
committees achieve little or nothing, and as this is
what they are created to achieve almost everyone is
satisfied. For a short while in the late seventies he
looked as if he might put his weight behind a
movement which nearly separated Scotland from the
British Isles, but on second thoughts he left things
as they were. He is now far less absurd, attractive

and demonic than the almost irresistible young man who plotted to seize the world and its works in the nineteen sixties, but he is much more comfortable. At the age of forty he became 293rd Moderator of the General Assembly of the United Seceders Free Presbyterian Church of Scotland and married a girl less than half his age who bore him six children, none of whom are very happy.

Jake and Jill neither married nor separated. Jake soon left bus conducting but took a teaching job in a London art school and came to enjoy it, for though a bad painter he is a good teacher. He is still sometimes unfaithful to Jill, being too gallant to repel all attempts to seduce him, but he never now hits or hurts her in any other way, no matter what she says or does. They have a flat in Ladbroke Grove where Jill has stopped sucking her thumb, grown interested in cooking and become plump, for she is too lazy to be influenced by the women's liberation movement. In their late thirties she and Jake had a child almost (but not quite) by accident, then got another by adopting the wholly accidental child of a friend.

These children are often happy.

It is easier for them.

They are English.

GOODBYE

Selected Grove Press Paperbacks

62334-7   ACKER, KATHY / Blood and Guts in High School / $7.95

62480-7   ACKER, KATHY / Great Expectations: A Novel / $6.95

62192-1   ALIFANO, ROBERTO / Twenty-four Conversations with Borges, 1980-1983 / $8.95

17458-5   ALLEN, DONALD & BUTTERICK, GEORGE F., eds. / The Postmoderns: The New American Poetry Revised 1945-1960 / $12.95

17801-7   ALLEN, DONALD M., & TALLMAN, WARREN, eds. / Poetics of the New American Poetry / $14.95

17061-X   ARDEN, JOHN / Arden: Plays One (Sergeant Musgrave's Dance, The Workhouse Donkey, Armstrong's Last Goodnight) / $4.95

17657-X   ARSAN, EMMANUELLE / Emmanuelle / $3.95

17213-2   ARTAUD, ANTONIN / The Theater and Its Double / $7.95

62433-5   BARASH, D. and LIPTON, J. / Stop Nuclear War! A Handbook / $7.95

62056-9   BARRY, TOM, WOOD, BETH & PREUSCH, DEB / The Other Side of Paradise: Foreign Control in the Caribbean / $11.95

17087-3   BARNES, JOHN / Evita—First Lady: A Biography of Eva Peron / $5.95

17928-5   BECKETT, SAMUEL / Company / $3.95

62489-0   BECKETT, SAMUEL / Disjecta: Miscellaneous Writings and a Dramatic Fragment, ed. Cohn, Ruby / $5.95

17208-6   BECKETT, SAMUEL / Endgame / $3.95

17953-6   BECKETT, SAMUEL / Ill Seen Ill Said / $4.95

62061-5   BECKETT, SAMUEL / Ohio Impromptu, Catastrophe, and What Where: Three Plays / $4.95

17924-2   BECKETT, SAMUEL / Rockababy and Other Short Pieces / $3.95

17299-X   BECKETT, SAMUEL / Three Novels: Molloy, Malone Dies and The Unnamable / $7.95

13034-8   BECKETT, SAMUEL / Waiting for Godot / $4.95

62418-1   BERLIN, NORMAND / Eugene O'Neill / $9.95

17237-X   BIELY, ANDREW / St. Petersburg / $12.50

17252-3   BIRCH, CYRIL & KEENE, DONALD, eds. / Anthology of Chinese Literature,Vol. I: From Early Times to the 14th Century / $17.50

17766-5   BIRCH, CYRIL, ed. / Anthology of Chinese Literature, Vol. II: From the 14th Century to the Present / $12.95

62104-2   BLOCH, DOROTHY / "So the Witch Won't Eat Me," Fantasy and the Child's Fear of Infanticide / $7.95

13030-5   BORGES, JORGE LUIS / Ficciones / $6.95

17270-1   BORGES, JORGE LUIS / A Personal Anthology / $6.95

62372-X	BRECHT, BERTOLT / The Caucasian Chalk Circle / $5.95
17109-8	BRECHT, BERTOLT / The Good Woman of Setzuan / $4.50
17112-8	BRECHT, BERTOLT / Galileo / $4.95
17065-2	BRECHT, BERTOLT / The Mother / $7.95
17106-3	BRECHT, BERTOLT / Mother Courage and Her Children / $3.95
17472-0	BRECHT, BERTOLT / Threepenny Opera / $3.95
17393-7	BRETON ANDRE / Nadja / $6.95
13011-9	BULGAKOV, MIKHAIL / The Master and Margarita / $6.95
17108-X	BURROUGHS, WILLIAM S. / Naked Lunch / $4.95
17749-5	BURROUGHS, WILLIAM S. / The Soft Machine, Nova Express, The Wild Boys: Three Novels / $5.95
62488-2	CLARK, AL, ed. / The Film Year Book 1984 / $12.95
17038-5	CLEARY, THOMAS / The Original Face: An Anthology of Rinzai Zen / $4.95
17735-5	CLEVE, JOHN / The Crusader Books I and II / $5.95
17411-9	CLURMAN, HAROLD (Ed.) / Nine Plays of the Modern Theater (Waiting for Godot by Samuel Beckett, The Visit by Friedrich Durrenmatt, Tango by Slawomir Mrozek, The Caucasian Chalk Circle by Bertolt Brecht, The Balcony by Jean Genet, Rhinoceros by Eugene Ionesco, American Buffalo by David Mamet, The Birthday Party by Harold Pinter, Rosencrantz and Guildenstern Are Dead by Tom Stoppard) / $15.95
17962-5	COHN, RUBY / New American Dramatists: 1960-1980 / $7.95
17971-4	COOVER, ROBERT / Spanking the Maid / $4.95
17535-1	COWARD, NOEL / Three Plays by Noel Coward (Private Lives, Hay Fever, Blithe Spirit) / $7.95
17740-1	CRAFTS, KATHY & HAUTHER, BRENDA / How To Beat the System: The Student's Guide to Good Grades / $3.95
17219-1	CUMMINGS, E.E. / 100 Selected Poems / $5.50
17329-5	DOOLITTLE, HILDA / Selected Poems of H.D. / $9.95
17863-7	DOSS, MARGOT PATTERSON / San Francisco at Your Feet (Second Revised Edition) / $8.95
17398-8	DOYLE, RODGER, & REDDING, JAMES / The Complete Food Handbook (revised any updated edition) / $3.50
17987-0	DURAS, MARGUERITE / Four Novels: The Afternoon of Mr. Andesmas; 10:30 on a Summer Night; Moderato Cantabile; The Square) / $9.95
17246-9	DURRENMATT, FRIEDRICH / The Physicists / $6.95
17239-6	DURRENMATT, FRIEDRICH / The Visit / $5.95
17990-0	FANON, FRANZ / Black Skin, White Masks / $8.95
17327-9	FANON, FRANZ / The Wretched of the Earth / $6.95
17754-1	FAWCETT, ANTHONY / John Lennon: One Day At A Time, A Personal Biography (Revised Edition) / $8.95
17902-1	FEUERSTEIN, GEORG / The Essence of Yoga / $3.95

62455-6	FRIED, GETTLEMAN, LEVENSON & PECKENHAM, eds. / Guatemala in Rebellion: Unfinished History / $8.95
17483-6	FROMM, ERICH / The Forgotten Language / $8.95
62073-9	GARWOOD, DARRELL / Under Cover: Thirty-five Years of CIA Deception / $3.95
17222-1	GELBER, JACK / The Connection / $3.95
17390-2	GENET, JEAN / The Maids and Deathwatch: Two Plays / $8.95
17470-4	GENET, JEAN / The Miracle of the Rose / $7.95
13013-5	GENET, JEAN / Our Lady of the Flowers / $8.95
62345-2	GETTLEMAN, LACEFIELD, MENASHE, MERMELSTEIN, & RADOSH, eds. / El Salvador: Central America in the New Cold War / $12.95
17994-3	GIBBS, LOIS MARIE / Love Canal: My Story / $6.95
17648-0	GIRODIAS, MAURICE, ed. / The Olympia Reader / $5.95
17067-9	GOMBROWICZ, WITOLD / Three Novels: Ferdydurke, Pornografia and Cosmos / $12.50
17764-9	GOVER, ROBERT / One Hundred Dollar Misunderstanding / $2.95
17832-7	GREENE, GERALD and CAROLINE / SM: The Last Taboo / $2.95
62490-4	GUITAR PLAYER MAGAZINE / The Guitar Player Book (Revised and Updated Edition) $11.95
17124-1	HARRIS, FRANK / My Life and Loves / $9.95
17936-6	HARWOOD, RONALD / The Dresser / $5.95
17653-7	HAVEL, VACLAV, The Memorandum / $5.95
17022-9	HAYMAN, RONALD / How To Read A Play / $6.95
17125-X	HOCHHUTH, ROLF / The Deputy / $7.95
62115-8	HOLMES, BURTON / The Olympian Games in Athens: The First Modern Olympics, 1896 / $6.95
17241-8	HUMPHREY, DORIS / The Art of Making Dances / $9.95
17075-X	INGE, WILLIAM / Four Plays (Come Back, Little Sheba; Picnic; Bus Stop; The Dark at the Top of the Stairs) / $8.95
62199-9	IONESCO, EUGENE / Exit the King, The Killer, Macbeth / $9.95
17209-4	IONESCO, EUGENE / Four Plays (The Bald Soprano, The Lesson, The Chairs, and Jack or The Submission) / $6.95
17226-4	IONESCO, EUGENE / Rhinoceros and Other Plays / $6.95
17485-2	JARRY, ALFRED / The Ubu Plays (Ubu Rex, Ubu Cuckolded, Ubu Enchained) / $9.95
62123-9	JOHNSON, CHARLES / Oxherding Tale / $6.95
62124-7	JORGENSEN, ELIZABETH WATIKINS & HENRY IRVIN / Eric Berne, Master Gamesman: A Transactional Biography / $9.95
17200-0	KEENE, DONALD, ed. / Japanese Literature: An Introduction for Western Readers-$2.25
17221-3	KEENE, DONALD, ed. / Anthology of Japanese Literature: Earliest Era to Mid-19th Century / $13.95

17278-7	KEROUAC, JACK / Dr. Sax / $5.95
17171-3	KEROUAC, JACK / Lonesome Traveler / $5.95
17287-6	KEROUAC, JACK / Mexico City Blues / $9.95
62173-5	KEROUAC, JACK / Satori in Paris / $4.95
17035-0	KERR, CARMEN / Sex for Women Who Want to Have Fun and Loving Relationships With Equals / $9.95
17981-1	KINGSLEY, PHILIP / The Complete Hair Book: The Ultimate Guide to Your Hair's Health and Beauty / $10.95
62424-6	LAWRENCE, D.H. / Lady Chatterley's Lover / $3.95
17178-0	LESTER, JULIUS / Black Folktales / $5.95
17481-X	LEWIS, MATTHEW / The Monk / $12.50
17391-0	LINSSEN, ROBERT / Living Zen / $12.50
17114-4	MALCOLM X (Breitman., ed.) / Malcolm X Speaks / $6.95
17023-7	MALRAUX, ANDRE/The Conquerors/$3.95
17068-7	MALRAUX, ANDRE/Lazarus/$2.95
17093-8	MALRAUX, ANDRE / Man's Hope / $12.50
17016-4	MAMET, DAVID / American Buffalo / $5.95
62049-6	MAMET, DAVID / Glengarry Glenn Ross / $6.95
17040-7	MAMET, DAVID / A Life in the Theatre / $9.95
17043-1	MAMET, DAVID / Sexual Perversity in Chicago & The Duck Variations / $7.95
17471-2	MILLER, HENRY / Black Spring / $4.95
62375-4	MILLER, HENRY / Tropic of Cancer / $7.95
62379-7	MILLER, HENRY / Tropic of Capricorn / $7.95
17933-1	MROZEK, SLAWOMIR / Three Plays: Striptease, Tango, Vatzlav / $12.50
13035-6	NERUDA, PABLO / Five Decades: Poems 1925-1970. bilingual ed. / $14.50
62243-X	NICOSIA, GERALD / Memory Babe: A Critical Biography of Jack Kerouac / $11.95
17092-X	ODETS, CLIFFORD / Six Plays (Waiting for Lefty, Awake and Sing, Golden Boy, Rocket to the Moon, Till the Day I Die, Paradise Lost) / $7.95
17650-2	OE, KENZABURO / A Personal Matter / $6.95
17002-4	OE, KENZABURO / Teach Us To Outgrow Our Madness (The Day He Himself Shall Wipe My Tears Away; Prize Stock; Teach Us to Outgrow Our Madness; Aghwee The Sky Monster) / $4.95
17992-7	PAZ, OCTAVIO / The Labyrinth of Solitude / $10.95
17084-9	PINTER, HAROLD / Betrayal / $6.95
17232-9	PINTER, HAROLD / The Birthday Party & The Room / $6.95
17251-5	PINTER, HAROLD / The Homecoming / $5.95
17539-5	POMERANCE / The Elephant Man / $5.95
62013-9	PORTWOOD, DORIS / Common Sense Suicide: The Final Right / $8.00

13021-6 WALEY, ARTHUR / The Book of Songs / $8.95
17211-6 WALEY, ARTHUR / Monkey / $8.95
17207-8 WALEY, ARTHUR / The Way and Its Power: A Study of the Tao
         Te Ching and Its Place in Chinese Thought / $9.95
17418-6 WATTS, ALAN W. / The Spirit of Zen / $6.95
62031-3 WORTH, KATHERINE / Oscar Wilde / $8.95
17739-8 WYCKOFF, HOGIE / Solving Problems Together / $7.95

GROVE PRESS, INC., 920 Broadway, New York, N.Y. 10010